**Robert Barr** (16 September 1849 – 21 October 1912) was a Scottish-Canadian short story writer and novelist. Robert Barr was born in Barony, Lanark, Scotland to Robert Barr and Jane Watson. In 1854, he emigrated with his parents to Upper Canada at the age of four years old. His family settled on a farm near the village of Muirkirk. Barr assisted his father with his job as a carpenter, and developed a sound work ethic. Robert Barr then worked as a steel smelter for a number of years before he was educated at Toronto Normal School in 1873 to train as a teacher. After graduating Toronto Normal School, Barr became a teacher, and eventually headmaster/principal of the Central School of Windsor, Ontario in 1874. While Barr worked as head master of the Central School of Windsor, Ontario, he began to contribute short stories—often based on personal experiences, and recorded his work. On August 1876, when he was 27, Robert Barr married Ontario-born Eva Bennett, who was 21. (Source: Wikipedia)

**Literary works:**
"The Face And The Mask" (1894)
In the Midst of Alarms (1894, 1900, 1912)
From Whose Bourne (1896)
One Day's Courtship (1896)
Revenge!
The Strong Arm
A Woman Intervenes (1896)
Tekla: A Romance of Love and War (1898)
Jennie Baxter, Journalist (1899)
The Unchanging East (1900)
The Victors (1901)
A Prince of Good Fellows (1902)
Over The Border: A Romance (1903)
The O'Ruddy, A Romance, with Stephen Crane (1903)

# A ROCK IN THE BALTIC

## ROBERT BARR

PRINCE CLASSICS

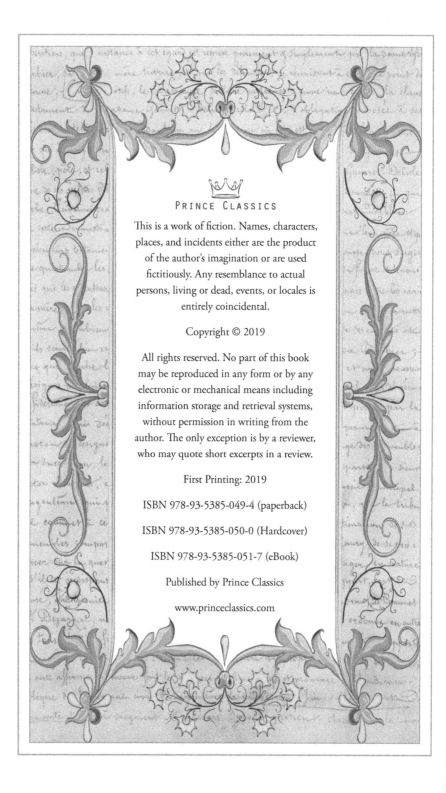

PRINCE CLASSICS

First Printing: 2019

ISBN 978-93-5385-049-4 (paperback)

ISBN 978-93-5385-050-0 (Hardcover)

ISBN 978-93-5385-051-7 (eBook)

Published by Prince Classics

www.princeclassics.com

# Contents

CHAPTER I —THE INCIDENT AT THE BANK ......................... 9

CHAPTER II —IN THE SEWING-ROOM ............................ 25

CHAPTER III —ON DECK ...................................... 37

CHAPTER IV —"AT LAST ALONE" ............................... 50

CHAPTER V —AFTER THE OPERA IS OVER ........................ 56

CHAPTER VI —FROM SEA TO MOUNTAIN ......................... 63

CHAPTER VII —"A WAY THEY HAVE IN THE NAVY" ................. 74

CHAPTER VIII —"WHEN JOHNNY COMES MARCHING HOME" ......... 83

CHAPTER IX —IN RUSSIA ..................................... 91

CHAPTER X —CALAMITY UNSEEN ............................... 97

CHAPTER XI —THE SNOW .................................... 104

CHAPTER XII —THE DREADED TROGZMONDOFF ................. 110

CHAPTER XIII —ENTRAPPED ................................. 121

CHAPTER XIV —A VOYAGE INTO THE UNKNOWN ............... 130

CHAPTER XV —"A HOME ON THE ROLLING DEEP" .............. 139

CHAPTER XVI —CELL NUMBER NINE .......................... 147

CHAPTER XVII —A FELLOW SCIENTIST ........................ 155

CHAPTER XVIII —CELL NUMBER ONE ......................... 161

CHAPTER XIX —"STONE WALLS DO NOT A PRISON MAKE" ....... 172

CHAPTER XX —ARRIVAL OF THE TURBINE YACHT .............. 181

CHAPTER XXI —THE ELOPEMENT ............................. 192

About Author ............................................. 199

# A ROCK IN THE BALTIC

# CHAPTER I — THE INCIDENT AT THE BANK

IN the public room of the Sixth National Bank at Bar Harbor in Maine, Lieutenant Alan Drummond, H.M.S. "Consternation," stood aside to give precedence to a lady. The Lieutenant had visited the bank for the purpose of changing several crisp white Bank of England notes into the currency of the country he was then visiting. The lady did not appear to notice either his courtesy or his presence, and this was the more remarkable since Drummond was a young man sufficiently conspicuous even in a crowd, and he and she were, at that moment, the only customers in the bank. He was tall, well-knit and stalwart, blond as a Scandinavian, with dark blue eyes which he sometimes said jocularly were the colors of his university. He had been slowly approaching the cashier's window with the easy movement of a man never in a hurry, when the girl appeared at the door, and advanced rapidly to the bank counter with its brass wire screen surrounding the arched aperture behind which stood the cashier. Although very plainly attired, her gown nevertheless possessed a charm of simplicity that almost suggested complex Paris, and she wore it with that air of distinction the secret of which is supposed to be the exclusive property of French and American women.

The young man saw nothing of this, and although he appreciated the beauty of the girl, what struck him at that instant was the expression of anxiety on her face, whose apparently temporary pallor was accentuated by an abundance of dark hair. It seemed to him that she had resolutely set herself a task which she was most reluctant to perform. From the moment she entered the door her large, dark eyes were fixed almost appealingly on the cashier, and they beheld nothing else. Drummond, mentally slow as he usually was, came to the quick conclusion that this was a supreme moment in her life, on which perhaps great issues depended. He saw her left hand grasp the corner of the ledge in front of the cashier with a grip of nervous tension, as if the support thus attained was necessary to her. Her right hand trembled slightly as she passed an oblong slip of paper through the aperture to the calm and indifferent official.

"Will you give me the money for this check?" she asked in a low voice.

The cashier scrutinized the document for some time in silence. The signature appeared unfamiliar to him.

"One moment, madam," he said quietly, and retired to a desk in the back part of the bank, where he opened a huge book, turned over some leaves rapidly, and ran his finger down a page. His dilatory action seemed to increase the young woman's panic. Her pallor increased, and she swayed slightly, as if in danger of falling, but brought her right hand to the assistance of the left, and so steadied herself against the ledge of the cashier's counter.

"By Jove!" said the Lieutenant to himself, "there's something wrong here. I wonder what it is. Such a pretty girl, too!"

The cashier behind his screen saw nothing of this play of the emotions. He returned nonchalantly to his station, and asked, in commonplace tones:

"How will you have the money, madam?"

"Gold, if you please," she replied almost in a whisper, a rosy flush chasing the whiteness from her face, while a deep sigh marked the passing of a crisis.

At this juncture an extraordinary thing happened. The cashier counted out some golden coins, and passed them through the aperture toward their new owner.

"Thank you," said the girl. Then, without touching the money, she turned like one hypnotized, her unseeing eyes still taking no heed of the big Lieutenant, and passed rapidly out of the bank, The cashier paid no regard to this abandonment of treasure. He was writing some hieroglyphics on the cashed check.

"By Jove!" gasped the Lieutenant aloud, springing forward as he spoke, sweeping the coins into his hand, and bolting for the door. This was an action which would have awakened the most negligent cashier had he been in a trance. Automatically he whisked out a revolver which lay in an open drawer under his hand.

"Stop, you scoundrel, or I fire!" he shouted, but the Lieutenant had already disappeared. Quick as thought the cashier darted into the passage, and without waiting to unfasten the low door which separated the public and private rooms of the bank, leaped over it, and, bareheaded, gave chase. A British naval officer in uniform, rapidly overtaking a young woman, quite unconscious of his approach, followed by an excited, bareheaded man with a revolver in his grasp, was a sight which would quickly have collected a crowd almost anywhere, but it happened to be the lunch hour, and the inhabitants of that famous summer resort were in-doors; thus, fortunately, the street was deserted. The naval officer was there because the hour of the midday meal on board the cruiser did not coincide with lunch time on shore. The girl was there because it happened to be the only portion of the day when she could withdraw unobserved from the house in which she lived, during banking hours, to try her little agitating financial experiment. The cashier was there because the bank had no lunch hour, and because he had just witnessed the most suspicious circumstance that his constantly alert eye had ever beheld. Calm and imperturbable as a bank cashier may appear to the outside public, he is a man under constant strain during business hours. Each person with whom he is unacquainted that confronts him at his post is a possible robber who at any moment may attempt, either by violence or chicanery, to filch the treasure he guards. The happening of any event outside the usual routine at once arouses a cashier's distrust, and this sudden flight of a stranger with money which did not belong to him quite justified the perturbation of the cashier. From that point onward, innocence of conduct or explanation so explicit as to satisfy any ordinary man, becomes evidence of more subtle guilt to the mind of a bank official. The ordinary citizen, seeing the Lieutenant finally overtake and accost the hurrying girl, raise his cap, then pour into her outstretched hand the gold he had taken, would have known at once that here was an every-day exercise of natural politeness. Not so the cashier. The farther he got from the bank, the more poignantly did he realize that these two in front, both strangers to him, had, by their combined action, lured him, pistol and all, away from his post during the dullest hour of the day. It was not the decamping with those few pieces of gold which now troubled him: it was fear of what might be going on behind him. He was positive that these two had acted in conjunction. The uniform worn by the man did not impose upon

11

him. Any thief could easily come by a uniform, and, as his mind glanced rapidly backwards over the various points of the scheme, he saw how effectual the plan was: first, the incredible remissness of the woman in leaving her gold on the counter; second, the impetuous disappearance of the man with the money; and, third, his own heedless plunge into the street after them. He saw the whole plot in a flash: he had literally leaped into the trap, and during his five or ten minutes' absence, the accomplices of the pair might have overawed the unarmed clerks, and walked off with the treasure. His cash drawer was unlocked, and even the big safe stood wide open. Surprise had as effectually lured him away as if he had been a country bumpkin. Bitterly and breathlessly did he curse his own precipitancy. His duty was to guard the bank, yet it had not been the bank that was robbed, but, at best a careless woman who had failed to pick up her money. He held the check for it, and the loss, if any, was hers, not the bank's, yet here he was, running bareheaded down the street like a fool, and now those two stood quite calmly together, he handing her the money, and thus spreading a mantle of innocence over the vile trick. But whatever was happening in the bank, he would secure two of the culprits at least. The two, quite oblivious of the danger that threatened them, were somewhat startled by a panting man, trembling with rage, bareheaded, and flourishing a deadly weapon, sweeping down upon them.

"Come back to the bank instantly, you two!" he shouted.

"Why?" asked the Lieutenant in a quiet voice.

"Because I say so, for one thing."

"That reason is unanswerable," replied the Lieutenant with a slight laugh, which further exasperated his opponent. "I think you are exciting yourself unnecessarily. May I beg you to put that pistol in your pocket? On the cruiser we always cover up the guns when ladies honor us with their presence. You wish me to return because I had no authority for taking the money? Right: come along."

The cashier regarded this as bluff, and an attempt to give the woman opportunity to escape.

"You must come back also," he said to the girl.

"I'd rather not," she pleaded in a low voice, and it was hardly possible to have made a more injudicious remark if she had taken the whole afternoon to prepare.

Renewed determination shone from the face of the cashier.

"You must come back to the bank," he reiterated.

"Oh, I say," protested the Lieutenant, "you are now exceeding your authority. I alone am the culprit. The young lady is quite blameless, and you have no right to detain her for a moment."

The girl, who had been edging away and showing signs of flight, which the bareheaded man, visibly on the alert, leaned forward ready to intercept, seemed to make up her mind to bow to the inevitable. Ignoring the cashier, she looked up at the blond Lieutenant with a slight smile on her pretty lips.

"It was really all my fault at the beginning," she said, "and very stupid of me. I am slightly acquainted with the bank manager, and I am sure he will vouch for me, if he is there."

With that she turned and walked briskly toward the bank, at so rapid a pace as to indicate that she did not wish an escort. The bareheaded official found his anger unaccountably deserting him, while a great fear that he had put his foot in it took its place.

"Really," said the Lieutenant gently, as they strode along together, "an official in your position should be a good judge of human nature. How any sane person, especially a young man, can look at that beautiful girl and suspect her of evil, passes my comprehension. Do you know her?"

"No," said the cashier shortly. "Do you?"

The Lieutenant laughed genially.

"Still suspicious, eh?" he asked. "No, I don't know her, but to use a banking term, you may bet your bottom dollar I'm going to. Indeed, I am rather grateful to you for your stubbornness in forcing us to return. It's a quality I like, and you possess it in marvelous development, so I intend to stand by you when the managerial censure is due. I'm very certain I met your manager at the dinner they gave us last night. Mr. Morton, isn't he?"

"Yes," growled the cashier, in gruff despondency.

"Ah, that's awfully jolly. One of the finest fellows I've met in ten years. Now, the lady said she was acquainted with him, so if I don't wheedle an introduction out of him, it will show that a man at a dinner and a man in a bank are two different individuals. You were looking for plots; so there is mine laid bare to you. It's an introduction, not gold, I'm conspiring for."

The cashier had nothing further to say. When they entered the bank together he saw the clerks all busily at work, and knew that no startling event had happened during his absence. The girl had gone direct to the manager's room, and thither the young men followed her. The bank manager was standing at his desk, trying to preserve a severe financial cast of countenance, which the twinkle in his eyes belied. The girl, also standing, had evidently been giving him a rapid sketch of what had occurred, but now fell into silence when accuser and accomplice appeared.

The advent of the Englishman was a godsend to the manager. He was too courteous a gentleman to laugh in the face of a lady who very seriously was relating a set of incidents which appealed to his sense of humor, so the coming of the Lieutenant enabled him to switch off his mirth on another subject, and in reply to the officer's cordial "Good-morning, Mr. Morton," he replied:

"Why, Lieutenant, I'm delighted to see you. That was a very jolly song you sang for us last night: I'll never forget it. What do you call it? Whittington Fair?" And he laughed outright, as at a genial recollection.

The Lieutenant blushed red as a girl, and stammered:

"Really, Mr. Morton, you know, that's not according to the rules of evidence. When a fellow comes up for trial, previous convictions are never allowed to be mentioned till after the sentence. Whiddicomb Fair should not be held against me in the present crisis."

The manager chuckled gleefully. The cashier, when he saw how the land lay, had quietly withdrawn, closing the door behind him.

"Well, Lieutenant, I think I must have this incident cabled to Europe," said Morton, "so the effete nations of your continent may know that a plain bank cashier isn't afraid to tackle the British navy. Indeed, Mr. Drummond, if you read history, you will learn that this is a dangerous coast for your warships. It seems rather inhospitable that a guest of our town cannot pick all the gold he wants out of a bank, but a cashier has necessarily somewhat narrow views on the subject. I was just about to apologize to Miss Amhurst, who is a valued client of ours, when you came in, and I hope, Miss Amhurst"—he continued gravely, turning to the girl—"that you will excuse us for the inconvenience to which you have been put."

"Oh, it does not matter in the least," replied the young woman, with nevertheless a sigh of relief. "It was all my own fault in so carelessly leaving the money. Some time, when less in a hurry than I am at the present moment, I will tell you how I came to make the blunder."

Meanwhile the manager caught and interpreted correctly an imploring look from the Lieutenant.

"Before you go, Miss Amhurst, will you permit me to introduce to you my friend, Lieutenant Drummond, of H.M.S. 'Consternation.'"

This ritual to convention being performed, the expression on the girl's face showed the renewal of her anxiety to be gone, and as she turned to the door, the officer sprang forward and opened it for her. If the manager expected the young man to return, he was disappointed, for Drummond threw over his shoulder the hasty remark:

"I will see you at the Club this evening," whereupon the genial Morton, finding himself deserted, sat down in his swivel chair and laughed quietly to himself.

There was the slightest possible shade of annoyance on the girl's face as the sailor walked beside her from the door of the manager's room, through the public portion of the bank to the exit, and the young man noticing this, became momentarily tongue-tied, but nevertheless persisted, with a certain

15

awkward doggedness which was not going to allow so slight a hint that his further attendance was unnecessary, to baffle him. He did not speak until they had passed down the stone steps to the pavement, and then his utterance began with a half-embarrassed stammer, as if the shadow of displeasure demanded justification on his part.

"You—you see, Miss Amhurst, we have been properly introduced."

For the first time he heard the girl laugh, just a little, and the sound was very musical to him.

"The introduction was of the slightest," she said. "I cannot claim even an acquaintance with Mr. Morton, although I did so in the presence of his persistent subordinate. I have met the manager of the bank but once before, and that for a few moments only, when he showed me where to sign my name in a big book."

"Nevertheless," urged Drummond, "I shall defend the validity of that introduction against all comers. The head of a bank is a most important man in every country, and his commendation is really very much sought after."

"You appear to possess it. He complimented your singing, you know," and there was a roguish twinkle in the girl's eye as she glanced up sideways at him, while a smile came to her lips as she saw the color again mount to his cheeks. She had never before met a man who blushed, and she could not help regarding him rather as a big boy than a person to be taken seriously. His stammer became more pronounced.

"I—I think you are laughing at me, Miss Amhurst, and indeed I don't wonder at it, and I—I am afraid you consider me even more persistent than the cashier. But I did want to tell you how sorry I am to have caused you annoyance."

"Oh, you have not done so," replied the girl quickly. "As I said before, it was all my own fault in the beginning."

"No, I shouldn't have taken the gold. I should have come up with you, and told you that it still awaited you in the bank, and now I beg your permission to walk down the street with you, because if any one were looking at us from these windows, and saw us pursued by a bareheaded man with a revolver, they will now, on looking out again, learn that it is all right, and may even come to regard the revolver and the hatless one as an optical delusion."

Again the girl laughed.

"I am quite unknown in Bar Harbor, having fewer acquaintances than even a stranger like yourself, therefore so far as I am concerned it does not in the least matter whether any one saw us or not. We shall walk together, then, as far as the spot where the cashier overtook us, and this will give me an opportunity of explaining, if not of excusing, my leaving the money on the counter. I am sure my conduct must have appeared inexplicable both to you and the cashier, although, of course, you would be too polite to say so."

"I assure you, Miss Amhurst—"

"I know what you would say," she interrupted, with a vivacity which had not heretofore characterized her, "but, you see, the distance to the corner is short, and, as I am in a hurry, if you don't wish my story to be continued in our next—"

"Ah, if there is to be a next—" murmured the young man so fervently that it was now the turn of color to redden her cheeks.

"I am talking heedlessly," she said quickly. "What I want to say is this: I have never had much money. Quite recently I inherited what had been accumulated by a relative whom I never knew. It seemed so incredible, so strange—well, it seems incredible and strange yet—and I have been expecting to wake and find it all a dream. Indeed, when you overtook me at this spot where we now stand, I feared you had come to tell me it was a mistake; to hurl me from the clouds to the hard earth again."

"But it was just the reverse of that," he cried eagerly. "Just the reverse, remember. I came to confirm your dream, and you received from my hand the first of your fortune."

"Yes," she admitted, her eyes fixed on the sidewalk.

17

"I see how it was," he continued enthusiastically. "I suppose you had never drawn a check before."

"Never," she conceded.

"And this was merely a test. You set up your dream against the hard common sense of a bank, which has no dreams. You were to transform your vision into the actual, or find it vanish. When the commonplace cashier passed forth the coin, their jingle said to you, 'The supposed phantasy is real,' but the gold pieces themselves at that supreme moment meant no more to you than so many worthless counters, so you turned your back upon them."

She looked up at him, her eyes, though moist, illumined with pleasure inspired by the sympathy in his tones rather than the import of his words. The girl's life heretofore had been as scant of kindness as of cash, and there was a deep sincerity in his voice which was as refreshing to her lonesome heart as it was new to her experience. This man was not so stupid as he had pretended to be. He had accurately divined the inner meaning of what had happened. She had forgotten the necessity for haste which had been so importunate a few minutes before.

"You must be a mind-reader," she said.

"No, I am not at all a clever person," he laughed. "Indeed, as I told you, I am always blundering into trouble, and making things uncomfortable for my friends. I regret to say I am rather under a cloud just now in the service, and I have been called upon to endure the frown of my superiors."

"Why, what has happened?" she asked. After their temporary halt at the corner where they had been overtaken, they now strolled along together like old friends, her prohibition out of mind.

"Well, you see, I was temporarily in command of the cruiser coming down the Baltic, and passing an island rock a few miles away, I thought it would be a good opportunity to test a new gun that had been put aboard when we left England. The sea was very calm, and the rock most temptsome. Of course I knew it was Russian territory, but who could have imagined that such a point in space was inhabited by anything else than sea-gulls."

"What!" cried the girl, looking up at him with new interest. "You don't mean to say you are the officer that Russia demanded from England, and England refused to give up?"

"Oh, England could not give me up, of course, but she apologized, and assured Russia she had no evil intent. Still, anything that sets the diplomatists at work is frowned upon, and the man who does an act which his government is forced to disclaim becomes unpopular with his superiors."

"I read about it in the papers at the time. Didn't the rock fire back at you?"

"Yes, it did, and no one could have been more surprised than I when I saw the answering puff of smoke."

"How came a cannon to be there?"

"Nobody knows. I suppose that rock in the Baltic is a concealed fort, with galleries and gun-rooms cut in the stone after the fashion of our defences at Gibraltar. I told the court-martial that I had added a valuable bit of information to our naval knowledge, but I don't suppose this contention exercised any influence on the minds of my judges. I also called their attention to the fact that my shell had hit, while the Russian shot fell half a mile short. That remark nearly cost me my commission. A court-martial has no sense of humor."

"I suppose everything is satisfactorily settled now?"

"Well, hardly that. You see, Continental nations are extremely suspicious of Britain's good intentions, as indeed they are of the good intentions of each other. No government likes to have—well, what we might call a 'frontier incident' happen, and even if a country is quite in the right, it nevertheless looks askance at any official of its own who, through his stupidity, brings about an international complication. As concerns myself, I am rather under a cloud, as I told you. The court martial acquitted me, but it did so with reluctance and a warning. I shall have to walk very straight for the next year or two, and be careful not to stub my toe, for the eyes of the Admiralty are upon me. However, I think I can straighten this matter out. I have six months' leave

19

coming on shortly, which I intend to spend in St. Petersburg. I shall make it my business to see privately some of the officials in the Admiralty there, and when they realize by personal inspection what a well-intentioned idiot I am, all distrust will vanish."

"I should do nothing of the kind," rejoined the girl earnestly, quite forgetting the shortness of their acquaintance, as she had forgotten the flight of time, while on his part he did not notice any incongruity in the situation. "I'd leave well enough alone," she added.

"Why do you think that?" he asked.

"Your own country has investigated the matter, and has deliberately run the risk of unpleasantness by refusing to give you up. How, then, can you go there voluntarily? You would be acting in your private capacity directly in opposition to the decision arrived at by your government."

"Technically, that is so; still, England would not hold the position she does in the world to-day if her men had not often taken a course in their private capacity which the government would never have sanctioned. As things stand now, Russia has not insisted on her demand, but has sullenly accepted England's decision, still quite convinced that my act was not only an invasion of Russia's domain, but a deliberate insult; therefore the worst results of an inconsiderate action on my part remain. If I could see the Minister for Foreign Affairs, or the head of the Admiralty in St. Petersburg face to face for ten minutes, I'd undertake to remove that impression."

"You have great faith in your persuasive powers," she said demurely.

The Lieutenant began to stammer again.

"No, no, it isn't so much that, but I have great faith in the Russian as a judge of character. I suppose I am imagined to be a venomous, brow-beating, truculent Russophobe, who has maliciously violated their territory, flinging a shell into their ground and an insult into their face. They are quite sincere in this belief. I want to remove that impression, and there's nothing like an ocular demonstration. I like the Russians. One of my best friends is a Russian."

The girl shook her head.

"I shouldn't attempt it," she persisted. "Suppose Russia arrested you, and said to England, 'We've got this man in spite of you'?"

The Lieutenant laughed heartily.

"That is unthinkable: Russia wouldn't do such a thing. In spite of all that is said about the Russian Government, its members are gentlemen. Of course, if such a thing happened, there would be trouble. That is a point where we're touchy. A very cheap Englishman, wrongfully detained, may cause a most expensive campaign. Our diplomatists may act correctly enough, and yet leave a feeling of resentment behind. Take this very case. Britain says coldly to Russia:

"'We disclaim the act, and apologize.'

"Now, it would be much more to the purpose if she said genially:

"'We have in our employment an impetuous young fool with a thirst for information. He wished to learn how a new piece of ordnance would act, so fired it off with no more intention of striking Russia than of hitting the moon. He knows much more about dancing than about foreign affairs. We've given him a month's leave, and he will slip across privately to St. Petersburg to apologize and explain. The moment you see him you will recognize he is no menace to the peace of nations. Meanwhile, if you can inculcate in him some cold, calm common-sense before he returns, we'll be ever so much obliged.'"

"So you are determined to do what you think the government should have done."

"Oh, quite. There will be nothing frigidly official about my unauthorized mission. I have a cousin in the embassy at St. Petersburg, but I shan't go near him; neither shall I go to an hotel, but will get quiet rooms somewhere that I may not run the risk of meeting any chance acquaintances."

"It seems to me you are about to afford the Russian Government an excellent opportunity of spiriting you off to Siberia, and nobody would be the wiser."

21

Drummond indulged in the free-hearted laugh of a youth to whom life is still rather a good joke.

"I shouldn't mind studying the Siberian system from the inside if they allowed me to return before my leave was up. I believe that sort of thing has been exaggerated by sensational writers. The Russian Government would not countenance anything of the kind, and if the minor officials tried to play tricks, there's always my cousin in the background, and it would be hard luck if I couldn't get a line to him. Oh, there's no danger in my project!"

Suddenly the girl came to a standstill, and gave expression to a little cry of dismay.

"What's wrong?" asked the Lieutenant.

"Why, we've walked clear out into the country!"

"Oh, is that all? I hadn't noticed."

"And there are people waiting for me. I must run."

"Nonsense, let them wait."

"I should have been back long since."

They had turned, and she was hurrying.

"Think of your new fortune, Miss Amhurst, safely lodged in our friend Morton's bank, and don't hurry for any one."

"I didn't say it was a fortune: there's only ten thousand dollars there."

"That sounds formidable, but unless the people who are waiting for you muster more than ten thousand apiece, I don't think you should make haste on their account."

"It's the other way about, Mr. Drummond. Individually they are poorer than I, therefore I should have returned long ago. Now, I fear, they will be in a temper."

"Well, if anybody left me two thousand pounds, I'd take an afternoon off to celebrate. Here we are in the suburbs again. Won't you change your mind and your direction; let us get back into the country, sit down on the hillside, look at the Bay, and gloat over your wealth?"

Dorothy Amhurst shook her head and held out her hand.

"I must bid you good-by here, Lieutenant Drummond. This is my shortest way home."

"May I not accompany you just a little farther?"

"Please, no, I wish to go the rest of the way alone."

He held her hand, which she tried to withdraw, and spoke with animation.

"There's so much I wanted to say, but perhaps the most important is this: I shall see you the night of the 14th, at the ball we are giving on the 'Consternation'?"

"It is very likely," laughed the girl, "unless you overlook me in the throng. There will be a great mob. I hear you have issued many invitations."

"We hope all our friends will come. It's going to be a great function. Your Secretary of the Navy has promised to look in on us, and our Ambassador from Washington will be there. I assure you we are doing our best, with festooned electric lights, hanging draperies, and all that, for we want to make the occasion at least remotely worthy of the hospitality we have received. Of course you have your card, but I wish you hadn't, so that I might have the privilege of sending you one or more invitations."

"That would be quite unnecessary," said the girl, again with a slight laugh and heightened color.

"If any of your friends need cards of invitation, won't you let me know, so that I may send them to you?"

"I'm sure I shan't need any, but if I do, I promise to remember your kindness, and apply."

"It will be a pleasure for me to serve you. With whom shall you come? I

23

should like to know the name, in case I should miss you in the crowd."

"I expect to be with Captain Kempt, of the United States Navy."

"Ah," said the Lieutenant, with a note of disappointment in his voice which he had not the diplomacy to conceal. His hold of her hand relaxed, and she took the opportunity to withdraw it.

"What sort of a man is Captain Kempt? I shall be on the lookout for him, you know."

"I think he is the handsomest man I have ever seen, and I know he is the kindest and most courteous."

"Really? A young man, I take it?"

"There speaks the conceit of youth," said Dorothy, smiling. "Captain Kempt, U.S.N., retired. His youngest daughter is just two years older than myself."

"Oh, yes, Captain Kempt. I—I remember him now. He was at the dinner last night, and sat beside our captain. What a splendid story-teller he is!" cried the Lieutenant with honest enthusiasm.

"I shall tell him that, and ask him how he liked your song. Good-by," and before the young man could collect his thoughts to make any reply, she was gone.

Skimming lightly over the ground at first, she gradually slackened her pace, and slowed down to a very sober walk until she came to a three-storied so-called "cottage" overlooking the Bay, then with a sigh she opened the gate, and went into the house by the servant's entrance.

## CHAPTER II —IN THE SEWING-ROOM

THREE women occupied the sewing-room with the splendid outlook: a mother and her two daughters. The mother sat in a low rocking-chair, a picture of mournful helplessness, her hands listlessly resting on her lap, while tears had left their traces on her time-worn face. The elder daughter paced up and down the room as striking an example of energy and impatience as was the mother of despondency. Her comely brow was marred by an angry frown. The younger daughter stood by the long window, her forehead resting against the pane, while her fingers drummed idly on the window sill. Her gaze was fixed on the blue Bay, where rested the huge British warship "Consternation," surrounded by a section of the United States squadron seated like white swans in the water. Sails of snow glistened here and there on the bosom of the Bay, while motor-boats and what-not darted this way and that impudently among the stately ships of the fleet.

In one corner of the room stood a sewing-machine, and on the long table were piles of mimsy stuff out of which feminine creations are constructed. There was no carpet on the floor, and no ceiling overhead; merely the bare rafters and the boards that bore the pine shingles of the outer roof; yet this attic was notable for the glorious view to be seen from its window. It was an ideal workshop.

The elder girl, as she walked to and fro, spoke with nervous irritation in her voice.

"There is absolutely no excuse, mamma, and it's weakness in you to pretend that there may be. The woman has been gone for hours. There's her lunch on the table which has never been tasted, and the servant brought it up at twelve."

She pointed to a tray on which were dishes whose cold contents bore out the truth of her remark.

"Perhaps she's gone on strike," said the younger daughter, without removing her eyes from H.M.S. "Consternation." "I shouldn't wonder if we went downstairs again we'd find the house picketed to keep away blacklegs."

"Oh, you can always be depended on to talk frivolous nonsense," said her elder sister scornfully. "It's the silly sentimental fashion in which both you and father treat work-people that makes them so difficult to deal with. If the working classes were taught their place—"

"Working classes! How you talk! Dorothy is as much a lady as we are, and sometimes I think rather more of a lady than either of us. She is the daughter of a clergyman."

"So she says," sniffed the elder girl.

"Well, she ought to know," replied the younger indifferently.

"It's people like you who spoil dependents in her position, with your Dorothy this and Dorothy that. Her name is Amhurst."

"Christened Dorothy, as witness godfather and godmother," murmured the younger without turning her head.

"I think," protested their mother meekly, as if to suggest a compromise, and throw oil on the troubled waters, "that she is entitled to be called Miss Amhurst, and treated with kindness but with reserve."

"Tush!" exclaimed the elder indignantly, indicating her rejection of the compromise.

"I don't see," murmured the younger, "why you should storm, Sabina. You nagged and nagged at her until she'd finished your ball-dress. It is mamma and I that have a right to complain. Our dresses are almost untouched, while you can sail grandly along the decks of the 'Consternation' like a fully rigged yacht. There, I'm mixing my similes again, as papa always says. A yacht doesn't sail along the deck of a battleship, does it?"

"It's a cruiser," weakly corrected the mother, who knew something of naval affairs.

"Well, cruiser, then. Sabina is afraid that papa won't go unless we all have grand new dresses, but mother can put on her old black silk, and I am going if I have to wear a cotton gown."

"To think of that person accepting our money, and absenting herself in this disgraceful way!"

"Accepting our money! That shows what it is to have an imagination. Why, I don't suppose Dorothy has had a penny for three months, and you know the dress material was bought on credit."

"You must remember," chided the mother mildly, "that your father is not rich."

"Oh, I am only pleading for a little humanity. The girl for some reason has gone out. She hasn't had a bite to eat since breakfast time, and I know there's not a silver piece in her pocket to buy a bun in a milk-shop."

"She has no business to be absent without leave," said Sabina.

"How you talk! As if she were a sailor on a battleship—I mean a cruiser."

"Where can the girl have gone?" wailed the mother, almost wringing her hands, partially overcome by the crisis. "Did she say anything about going out to you, Katherine? She sometimes makes a confidant of you, doesn't she?"

"Confidant!" exclaimed Sabina wrathfully.

"I know where she has gone," said Katherine with an innocent sigh.

"Then why didn't you tell us before?" exclaimed mother and daughter in almost identical terms.

"She has eloped with the captain of the 'Consternation,'" explained Katherine calmly, little guessing that her words contained a color of truth. "Papa sat next him at the dinner last night, and says he is a jolly old salt and a bachelor. Papa was tremendously taken with him, and they discussed tactics together. Indeed, papa has quite a distinct English accent this morning, and I suspect a little bit of a headache which he tries to conceal with a wavering smile."

"You can't conceal a headache, because it's invisible," said the mother seriously. "I wish you wouldn't talk so carelessly, Katherine, and you mustn't speak like that of your father."

"Oh, papa and I understand one another," affirmed Katherine with great confidence, and now for the first time during this conversation the young girl turned her face away from the window, for the door had opened to let in the culprit.

"Now, Amhurst, what is the meaning of this?" cried Sabina before her foot was fairly across the threshold.

All three women looked at the newcomer. Her beautiful face was aglow, probably through the exertion of coming up the stairs, and her eyes shone like those of the Goddess of Freedom as she returned steadfastly the supercilious stare with which the tall Sabina regarded her.

"I was detained," she said quietly.

"Why did you go away without permission?"

"Because I had business to do which could not be transacted in this room."

"That doesn't answer my question. Why did you not ask permission?"

The girl slowly raised her two hands, and showed her shapely wrists close together, and a bit of the forearm not covered by the sleeve of her black dress.

"Because," she said slowly, "the shackles have fallen from these wrists."

"I'm sure I don't know what you mean," said Sabina, apparently impressed in spite of herself, but the younger daughter clapped her hands rapturously.

"Splendid, splendid, Dorothy," she cried. "I don't know what you mean either, but you look like Maxine Elliott in that play where she—"

"Will you keep quiet!" interrupted the elder sister over her shoulder.

"I mean that I intend to sew here no longer," proclaimed Dorothy.

"Oh, Miss Amhurst, Miss Amhurst," bemoaned the matron. "You will heartlessly leave us in this crisis when we are helpless; when there is not a sewing woman to be had in the place for love or money. Every one is working night and day to be ready for the ball on the fourteenth, and you—you whom we have nurtured—"

"I suppose she gets more money," sneered the elder daughter bitterly.

"Oh, Dorothy," said Katherine, coming a step forward and clasping her hands, "do you mean to say I must attend the ball in a calico dress after all? But I'm going, nevertheless, if I dance in a morning wrapper."

"Katherine," chided her mother, "don't talk like that."

"Of course, where more money is in the question, kindness does not count," snapped the elder daughter.

Dorothy Amhurst smiled when Sabina mentioned the word kindness.

"With me, of course, it's entirely a question of money," she admitted.

"Dorothy, I never thought it of you," said Katherine, with an exaggerated sigh. "I wish it were a fancy dress ball, then I'd borrow my brother Jack's uniform, and go in that."

"Katherine, I'm shocked at you," complained the mother.

"I don't care: I'd make a stunning little naval cadet. But, Dorothy, you must be starved to death; you've never touched your lunch."

"You seem to have forgotten everything to-day," said Sabina severely. "Duty and everything else."

"You are quite right," murmured Dorothy.

"And did you elope with the captain of the 'Consternation,' and were you married secretly, and was it before a justice of the peace? Do tell us all about it."

"What are you saying?" asked Dorothy, with a momentary alarm coming into her eyes.

"Oh, I was just telling mother and Sab that you had skipped by the

29

light of the noon, with the captain of the 'Consternation,' who was a jolly old bachelor last night, but may be a married man to-day if my suspicions are correct. Oh, Dorothy, must I go to the ball in a dress of print?"

The sewing girl bent an affectionate look on the impulsive Katherine.

"Kate, dear," she said, "you shall wear the grandest ball dress that ever was seen in Bar Harbor."

"How dare you call my sister Kate, and talk such nonsense?" demanded Sabina.

"I shall always call you Miss Kempt, and now, if I have your permission, I will sit down. I am tired."

"Yes, and hungry, too," cried Katherine. "What shall I get you, Dorothy? This is all cold."

"Thank you, I am not in the least hungry."

"Wouldn't you like a cup of tea?"

Dorothy laughed a little wearily.

"Yes, I would," she said, "and some bread and butter."

"And cake, too," suggested Katherine.

"And cake, too, if you please."

Katherine skipped off downstairs.

"Well, I declare!" ejaculated Sabina with a gasp, drawing herself together, as if the bottom had fallen out of the social fabric.

Mrs. Captain Kempt folded her hands one over the other and put on a look of patient resignation, as one who finds all the old landmarks swept away from before her.

"Is there anything else we can get for you?" asked Sabina icily.

"Yes," replied Dorothy, with serene confidence, "I should be very much obliged if Captain Kempt would obtain for me a card of invitation to the ball on the 'Consternation.'"

"Really!" gasped Sabina, "and may not my mother supplement my father's efforts by providing you with a ball dress for the occasion?"

"I could not think of troubling her, Miss Kempt. Some of my customers have flattered me by saying that my taste in dress is artistic, and that my designs, if better known, might almost set a fashion in a small way, so I shall look after my costume myself; but if Mrs. Captain Kempt were kind enough to allow me to attend the ball under her care, I should be very grateful for it."

"How admirable! And is there nothing that I can do to forward your ambitions, Miss Amhurst?"

"I am going to the ball merely as a looker-on, and perhaps you might smile at me as you pass by with your different partners, so that people would say I was an acquaintance of yours."

After this there was silence in the sewing room until Katherine, followed by a maid, entered with tea and cakes. Some dress materials that rested on a gypsy table were swept aside by the impulsive Katherine, and the table, with the tray upon it, was placed at the right hand of Dorothy Amhurst. When the servant left the room, Katherine sidled to the long sewing table, sprang up lightly upon it, and sat there swinging a dainty little foot. Sabina had seated herself in the third chair of the room, the frown still adding severity to an otherwise beautiful countenance. It was the younger daughter who spoke.

"Now, Dorothy, tell us all about the elopement."

"What elopement?"

"I soothed my mother's fears by telling her that you had eloped with the captain of the 'Consternation.' I must have been wrong in that guess, because if the secret marriage I hoped had taken place, you would have said to Sabina that the shackles were on your wrists instead of off. But something important has happened, and I want to know all about it."

Dorothy made no response to this appeal, and after a minute's silence

Sabina said practically:

"All that has happened is that Miss Amhurst wishes father to present her with a ticket to the ball on the 'Consternation,' and taking that for granted, she requests mother to chaperon her, and further expresses a desire that I shall be exceedingly polite to her while we are on board the cruiser."

"Oh," cried Katherine jauntily, "the last proviso is past praying for, but the other two are quite feasible. I'd be delighted to chaperon Dorothy myself, and as for politeness, good gracious, I'll be polite enough to make up for all the courteous deficiency of the rest of the family.

*'For I hold that on the seas,*

*The expression if you please*

*A particularly gentlemanly tone implants,*

*And so do his sisters and his cousins and his aunts.'*

Now, Dorothy, don't be bashful. Here's your sister and your cousin and your aunt waiting for the horrifying revelation. What has happened?"

"I'll tell you what is going to happen, Kate," said the girl, smiling at the way the other ran on. "Mrs. Captain Kempt will perhaps consent to take you and me to New York or Boston, where we will put up at the best hotel, and trick ourselves out in ball costumes that will be the envy of Bar Harbor. I shall pay the expense of this trip as partial return for your father's kindness in getting me an invitation and your mother's kindness in allowing me to be one of your party."

"Oh, then it isn't an elopement, but a legacy. Has the wicked but wealthy relative died?"

"Yes," said Dorothy solemnly, her eyes on the floor.

"Oh, I am so sorry for what I have just said!"

"You always speak without thinking," chided her mother.

"Yes, don't I? But, you see, I thought somehow that Dorothy had no relatives; but if she had one who was wealthy, and who allowed her to slave at sewing, then I say he was wicked, dead or alive, so there!"

"When work is paid for it is not slavery," commented Sabina with severity and justice.

The sewing girl looked up at her.

"My grandfather, in Virginia, owned slaves before the war, and I have often thought that any curse which may have been attached to slavery has at least partly been expiated by me, as foreshadowed in the Bible, where it says that the sins of the fathers shall affect the third or fourth generations. I was thinking of that when I spoke of the shackles falling from my wrists, for sometimes, Miss Kempt, you have made me doubt whether wages and slavery are as incompatible as you appear to imagine. My father, who was a clergyman, often spoke to me of his father's slaves, and while he never defended the institution, I think the past in his mind was softened by a glamor that possibly obscured the defects of life on the plantation. But often in depression and loneliness I have thought I would rather have been one of my grandfather's slaves than endure the life I have been called upon to lead."

"Oh, Dorothy, don't talk like that, or you'll make me cry," pleaded Kate. "Let us be cheerful whatever happens. Tell us about the money. Begin 'Once upon a time,' and then everything will be all right. No matter how harrowing such a story begins, it always ends with lashin's and lashin's of money, or else with a prince in a gorgeous uniform and gold lace, and you get the half of his kingdom. Do go on."

Dorothy looked up at her impatient friend, and a radiant cheerfulness chased away the gathering shadows from her face.

"Well, once upon a time I lived very happily with my father in a little rectory in a little town near the Hudson River. His family had been ruined by the war, and when the plantation was sold, or allowed to go derelict, whatever money came from it went to his elder and only brother. My father was a dreamy scholar and not a business man as his brother seems to have been. My mother had died when I was a child; I do not remember her. My

33

father was the kindest and most patient of men, and all I know he taught me. We were very poor, and I undertook the duties of housekeeper, which I performed as well as I was able, constantly learning by my failures. But my father was so indifferent to material comforts that there were never any reproaches. He taught me all that I know in the way of what you might call accomplishments, and they were of a strangely varied order—a smattering of Latin and Greek, a good deal of French, history, literature, and even dancing, as well as music, for he was an excellent musician. Our meager income ceased with my father's life, and I had to choose what I should do to earn my board and keep, like Orphant Annie, in Whitcomb Riley's poem. There appeared to be three avenues open to me. I could be a governess, domestic servant, or dressmaker. I had already earned something at the latter occupation, and I thought if I could set up in business for myself, there was a greater chance of gaining an independence along that line than either as a governess or servant. But to do this I needed at least a little capital.

"Although there had been no communication between the two brothers for many years, I had my uncle's address, and I wrote acquainting him with the fact of my father's death, and asking for some assistance to set up in business for myself, promising to repay the amount advanced with interest as soon as I was able, for although my father had never said anything against his elder brother, I somehow had divined, rather than knew, that he was a hard man, and his answering letter gave proof of that, for it contained no expression of regret for his brother's death. My uncle declined to make the advance I asked for, saying that many years before he had given my father two hundred dollars which had never been repaid. I was thus compelled, for the time at least, to give up my plan for opening a dressmaking establishment, even on the smallest scale, and was obliged to take a situation similar to that which I hold here. In three years I was able to save the two hundred dollars, which I sent to my uncle, and promised to remit the interest if he would tell me the age of the debt. He replied giving the information, and enclosing a receipt for the principal, with a very correct mathematical statement of the amount of interest if compounded annually, as was his legal right, but expressing his readiness to accept simple interest, and give me a receipt in full."

"The brute!" ejaculated Katherine, which remark brought upon her a mild rebuke from her mother on intemperance of language.

"Well, go on," said Katherine, unabashed.

"I merely mention this detail," continued Dorothy, "as an object lesson in honesty. Never before since the world began was there such a case of casting bread upon the waters as was my sending the two hundred dollars. My uncle appears to have been a most methodical man. He filed away my letter which contained the money, also a typewritten copy of his reply, and when he died, it was these documents which turned the attention of the legal arm who acted for him to myself, for my uncle had left no will. The Californian firm communicated with lawyers in New York, and they began a series of very cautious inquiries, which at last resulted, after I had furnished certain proofs asked for, in my being declared heiress to my uncle's estate."

"And how much did you get? How much did you get?" demanded Katherine.

"I asked the lawyers from New York to deposit ten thousand dollars for me in the Sixth National Bank of this town, and they did so. It was to draw a little check against that deposit, and thus learn if it was real, that I went out to-day."

"Ten thousand dollars," murmured Katherine, in accents of deep disappointment. "Is that all?"

"Isn't that enough?" asked Dorothy, with a twinkle in her eyes.

"No, you deserve ten times as much, and I'm not going to New York or Boston at your expense to buy new dresses. Not likely! I will attend the ball in my calico."

Dorothy laughed quietly, and drew from the little satchel she wore at her side a letter, which she handed to Katherine.

"It's private and confidential," she warned her friend.

"Oh, I won't tell any one," said Katherine, unfolding it. She read eagerly half-way down the page, then sprang to her feet on the top of the table, screaming:

"Fifteen million dollars! Fifteen million dollars!" and, swinging her arms back and forth like an athlete about to leap, sprang to the floor, nearly upsetting the little table, tray and all, as she embraced Dorothy Amhurst.

"Fifteen millions! That's something like! Why, mother, do you realize that we have under our roof one of the richest young women in the world? Don't you see that the rest of this conference must take place in our drawing-room under the most solemn auspices? The idea of our keeping such an heiress in the attic!"

"I believe," said Sabina, slowly and coldly, "that Mr. Rockefeller's income is—"

"Oh, blow Mr. Rockefeller and his income!" cried the indignant younger sister.

"Katherine!" pleaded the mother tearfully.

# CHAPTER III —ON DECK

THROUGHOUT the long summer day a gentle excitement had fluttered the hearts of those ladies, young, or not so young, who had received invitations to the ball on board the "Consternation" that night. The last touches were given to creations on which had been spent skill, taste, and money. Our three young women, being most tastefully and fashionably attired, were in high spirits, which state of feeling was exhibited according to the nature of each; Sabina rather stately in her exaltation; Dorothy quiet and demure; while Katherine, despite her mother's supplications, would not be kept quiet, but swung her graceful gown this way and that, practising the slide of a waltz, and quoting W. R. Gilbert, as was her custom. She glided over the floor in rhythm with her chant.

> "When I first put this uniform on
>
> I said, as I looked in the glass,
>
> 'It's one to a million
>
> That any civilian
>
> My figure and form will surpass.'"

Meanwhile, in a room downstairs that good-natured veteran Captain Kempt was telling the latest stories to his future son-in-law, a young officer of the American Navy, who awaited, with dutiful impatience, the advent of the serene Sabina. When at last the ladies came down the party set out through the gathering darkness of this heavenly summer night for the private pier from which they were privileged, because of Captain Kempt's official standing, to voyage to the cruiser on the little revenue cutter "Whip-poor-will," which was later on to convey the Secretary of the Navy and his entourage across the same intervening waters. Just before they reached the pier their steps were arrested by the boom of a cannon, followed instantly by the sudden apparition of the "Consternation" picked out in electric light; masts, funnel and hull all outlined by incandescent stars.

"How beautiful!" cried Sabina, whose young man stood beside her. "It is as if a gigantic racket, all of one color, had burst, and hung suspended there like the planets of heaven."

"It reminds me," whispered Katherine to Dorothy, "of an overgrown pop-corn ball," at which remark the two girls were frivolous enough to laugh.

"Crash!" sounded a cannon from an American ship, and then the white squadron became visible in a blaze of lightning. And now all the yachts and other craft on the waters flaunted their lines of fire, and the whole Bay was illuminated like a lake in Fairyland.

"Now," said Captain Kempt with a chuckle, "watch the Britisher. I think she's going to show us some color," and as he spoke there appeared, spreading from nest to mast, a huge sheet of blue, with four great stars which pointed the corners of a parallelogram, and between the stars shone a huge white anchor. Cheers rang out from the crew of the "Consternation," and the band on board played "The Star-Spangled Banner."

"That," said Captain Kempt in explanation, "is the flag of the United States Secretary of the Navy, who will be with us to-night. The visitors have kept very quiet about this bit of illumination, but our lads got on to the secret about a week ago, and I'll be very much disappointed if they don't give 'em tit for tat."

When the band on the "Consternation" ceased playing, all lights went out on the American squadron, and then on the flagship appeared from mast to mast a device with the Union Jack in the corner, a great red cross dividing the flag into three white squares. As this illumination flashed out the American band struck up the British national anthem, and the outline lights appeared again.

"That," said the captain, "is the British man-o'-war's flag."

The "Whip-poor-will" speedily whisked the party and others across the sparkling waters to the foot of the grand stairway which had been specially constructed to conduct the elect from the tide to the deck. It was more than double as broad as the ordinary gangway, was carpeted from top to bottom,

38

and on every step stood a blue-jacket, each as steady as if cast in bronze, the line forming, as one might say, a living handrail rising toward the dark sky.

Captain Kempt and his wife went first, followed by Sabina and her young man with the two girls in their wake.

"Aren't those men splendid?" whispered Katherine to her friend. "I wish each held an old-fashioned torch. I do love a sailor."

"So do I," said Dorothy, then checked herself, and laughed a little.

"I guess we all do," sighed Katherine.

On deck the bluff captain of the "Consternation," in resplendent uniform, stood beside Lady Angela Burford of the British Embassy at Washington, to receive the guests of the cruiser. Behind these two were grouped an assemblage of officers and very fashionably dressed women, chatting vivaciously with each other. As Dorothy looked at the princess-like Lady Angela it seemed as if she knew her; as if here were one who had stepped out of an English romance. Her tall, proudly held figure made the stoutish captain seem shorter than he actually was. The natural haughtiness of those classic features was somewhat modified by a pro tem smile. Captain Kempt looked back over his shoulder and said in a low voice:

"Now, young ladies, best foot forward. The Du Maurier woman is to receive the Gibson girls."

"I know I shall laugh, and I fear I shall giggle," said Katherine, but she encountered a glance from her elder sister quite as haughty as any Lady Angela might have bestowed, and all thought of merriment fled for the moment; thus the ordeal passed conventionally without Katherine either laughing or giggling.

Sabina and her young man faded away into the crowd. Captain Kempt was nodding to this one and that of his numerous acquaintances, and Katherine felt Dorothy shrink a little closer to her as a tall, unknown young man deftly threaded his way among the people, making directly for the Captain, whom he seized by the hand in a grasp of the most cordial friendship.

"Captain Kempt, I am delighted to meet you again. My name is Drummond—Lieutenant Drummond, and I had the pleasure of being introduced to you at that dinner a week or two ago."

"The pleasure was mine, sir, the pleasure was mine," exclaimed the Captain with a cordiality equal to that with which he had been greeted. He had not at first the least recollection of the young man, but the Captain was something of an amateur politician, and possessed all a politician's expertness in facing the unknown, and making the most of any situation in which he found himself.

"Oh, yes, Lieutenant, I remember very well that excellent song you—"

"Isn't it a perfect night?" gasped the Lieutenant. "I think we are to be congratulated on our weather."

He still clung to the Captain's hand, and shook it again so warmly that the Captain said to himself:

"I must have made an impression on this young fellow," then aloud he replied jauntily:

"Oh, we always have good weather this time of year. You see, the United States Government runs the weather. Didn't you know that? Yes, our Weather Bureau is considered the best in the world."

The Lieutenant laughed heartily, although a hollow note intervened, for the young man had got to the end of his conversation, realized he could not shake hands for a third time, yet did not know what more to say. The suavity of the politician came to his rescue in just the form the Lieutenant had hoped.

"Lieutenant Drummond, allow me to introduce my wife to you."

The lady bowed.

"And my daughter, Katherine, and Miss Amhurst, a friend of ours—Lieutenant Drummond, of the 'Consternation.'"

"I wonder," said the Lieutenant, as if the thought had just occurred to him, "if the young ladies would like to go to a point where they can have a

40

comprehensive view of the decorations. I—I may not be the best guide, but I am rather well acquainted with the ship, you know."

"Don't ask me," said Captain Kempt. "Ask the girls. Everything I've had in life has come to me because I asked, and if I didn't get it the first time, I asked again."

"Of course we want to see the decorations," cried Katherine with enthusiasm, and so bowing to the Captain and Mrs. Kempt, the Lieutenant led the young women down the deck, until he came to an elevated spot out of the way of all possible promenaders, on which had been placed in a somewhat secluded position, yet commanding a splendid view of the throng, a settee with just room for two, that had been taken from some one's cabin. A blue-jacket stood guard over it, but at a nod from the Lieutenant he disappeared.

"Hello!" cried Katherine, "reserved seats, eh? How different from a theatre chair, where you are entitled to your place by holding a colored bit of cardboard. Here a man with a cutlass stands guard. It gives one a notion of the horrors of war, doesn't it, Dorothy?"

The Lieutenant laughed quite as heartily as if he had not himself hoped to occupy the position now held by the sprightly Katherine. He was cudgelling his brain to solve the problem represented by the adage "Two is company, three is none." The girls sat together on the settee and gazed out over the brilliantly lighted, animated throng. People were still pouring up the gangways, and the decks were rapidly becoming crowded with a many-colored, ever-shifting galaxy of humanity. The hum of conversation almost drowned the popular selections being played by the cruiser's excellent band. Suddenly one popular selection was cut in two. The sound of the instruments ceased for a moment, then they struck up "The Stars and Stripes for Ever."

"Hello," cried Katherine, "can your band play Sousa?"

"I should say we could," boasted the Lieutenant, "and we can play his music, in a way to give some hints to Mr. Sousa's own musicians."

"To beat the band, eh?—Sousa's band?" rejoined Katherine, dropping into slang.

"Exactly," smiled the Lieutenant, "and now, young ladies, will you excuse me for a few moments? This musical selection means that your Secretary of the Navy is on the waters, and I must be in my place with the rest of the officers to receive him and his staff with all ceremony. Please promise you will not leave this spot till I return: I implore you."

"Better put the blue-jacket on guard over us," laughed Katherine.

"By Jove! a very good idea."

Dorothy saw all levity depart from his face, giving way to a look of sternness and command. Although he was engaged in a joke, the subordinate must see no sign of fooling in his countenance. He said a sharp word to a blue-jacket, who nimbly sprang to the end of the settee, raised his hand in salute, and stiffened himself to an automaton. Then the girls saw the tall figure of the Lieutenant wending its way to the spot where the commander stood.

"I say, Dorothy, we're prisoners. I wonder what this Johnny would do if we attempted to fly. Isn't the Lieutenant sumptuous?"

"He seems a very agreeable person," murmured Dorothy.

"Agreeable! Why, he's splendid. I tell you, Dorothy, I'm going to have the first dance with him. I'm the eldest. He's big enough to divide between two small girls like us, you know."

"I don't intend to dance," said Dorothy.

"Nonsense, you're not going to sit here all night with nobody to speak to. I'll ask the Lieutenant to bring you a man. He'll take two or three blue-jackets and capture anybody you want."

"Katherine," said Dorothy, almost as severely as if it were the elder sister who spoke, "if you say anything like that, I'll go back to the house."

"You can't get back. I'll appeal to the guard. I'll have you locked up if you don't behave yourself."

"You should behave yourself. Really, Katherine, you must be careful what you say, or you'll make me feel very unhappy."

Katherine caught her by the elbow, and gave it an affectionate little squeeze.

"Don't be frightened, Miss Propriety, I wouldn't make you unhappy for the world. But surely you're going to dance?"

Dorothy shook her head.

"Some other time. Not to-night. There are too many people here. I shouldn't enjoy it, and—there are other reasons. This is all so new and strange to me: these brilliant men and beautiful women—the lights, the music, everything—it is as if I had stepped into another world; something I had read about, or perhaps dreamed about, and never expected to see."

"Why, you dear girl, I'm not going to dance either, then."

"Oh, yes, you will, Katherine; you must."

"I couldn't be so selfish as to leave you here all alone."

"It isn't selfish at all, Katherine. I shall enjoy myself completely here. I don't really wish to talk to any one, but simply to enjoy my dream, with just a little fear at the bottom of my heart that I shall suddenly wake up, rubbing my eyes, in the sewing room."

Katherine pinched her.

"Now are you awake?"

Dorothy smiled, still dreaming.

"Hello!" cried Katherine, with renewed animation, "they've got the Secretary safe aboard the lugger, and they seem to be clearing the decks for action. Here is my dear Lieutenant returning; tall even among tall men. Look at him. He's in a great hurry, yet so polite, and doesn't want to bump against anybody. And now, Dorothy, don't you be afraid. I shall prove a perfect model of diffidence. You will be proud of me when you learn with what timidity I pronounce prunes and prism. I think I must languish a little at him. I don't know quite how it's done, but in old English novels the girls always languished, and perhaps an Englishman expects a little languishment in his. I wonder if he comes of a noble family. If he doesn't, I don't think I'll languish very much. Still, what matters the pomp of pageantry and pride of race—isn't that the way the poem runs? I love our dear little Lieutenant for himself alone, and I think I will have just one dance with him, at least."

Drummond had captured a camp-stool somewhere, and this he placed at right angles to the settee, so that he might face the two girls, and yet not interrupt their view. The sailor on guard once more faded away, and the band now struck up the music of the dance.

"Well," cried Drummond cheerfully, "I've got everything settled. I've received the Secretary of the Navy: our captain is to dance with his wife, and the Secretary is Lady Angela's partner. There they go!"

For a few minutes the young people watched the dance, then the Lieutenant said:

"Ladies, I am disappointed that you have not complimented our electrical display."

"I am sure it's very nice, indeed, and most ingenious," declared Dorothy, speaking for the first time that evening to the officer, but Katherine, whose little foot was tapping the deck to the dance music, tossed her head, and declared nonchalantly that it was all very well as a British effort at illumination, but she begged the young man to remember that America was the home of electricity.

"Where would you have been if it were not for Edison?"

"I suppose," said the Lieutenant cheerfully, "that we should have been where Moses was when the candle went out—in the dark."

"You might have had torches," said Dorothy. "My friend forgets she was wishing the sailors held torches on that suspended stairway up the ship's side."

"I meant electric torches—Edison torches, of course."

Katherine was displeased at the outlook. She was extremely fond of dancing, and here this complacent young man had planted himself down on a camp stool to talk of electricity.

"Miss Kempt, I am sorry that you are disappointed at our display. Your slight upon British electrical engineering leaves us unscathed, because this has been done by a foreign mechanic, whom I wish to present to you."

"Oh, indeed," said Katherine, rather in the usual tone of her elder sister. "I don't dance with mechanics, thank you."

She emphasized the light fantastic word, but the Lieutenant did not take the hint; he merely laughed again in an exasperatingly good-natured way, and said:

"Lady Angela is going to be Jack Lamont's partner for the next waltz."

"Oh," said Katherine loftily, "Lady Angela may dance with any blacksmith that pleases her, but I don't. I'm taking it for granted that Jack Lamont is your electrical tinsmith."

"Yes, he is, and I think him by all odds the finest fellow aboard this ship. It's quite likely you have read about his sister. She is a year older than Jack, very beautiful, cultured, everything that a grande dame should be, yet she has given away her huge estate to the peasantry, and works with them in the fields, living as they do, and faring as they do. There was an article about her in one of the French reviews not long ago. She is called the Princess Natalia."

"The Princess Natalia!" echoed Katherine, turning her face toward the young man. "How can Princess Natalia be a sister of Jack Lamont? Did she marry some old prince, and take to the fields in disgust?"

"Oh, no; Jack Lamont is a Russian. He is called Prince Ivan Lermontoff when he's at home, but we call him Jack Lamont for short. He's going to help me on the Russian business I told you of."

"What Russian business?" asked Katherine. "I don't remember your speaking of it."

Dorothy went white, edged a little way from her friend, while her widening eyes flashed a warning at the Lieutenant, who, too late, remembered that this conversation on Russia had taken place during the walk from the bank. The young man coughed slightly behind his open hand, reddened, and stammered:

"Oh, I thought I had told you. Didn't I mention the prince to you as we were coming here?"

"Not that I recollect," said Katherine. "Is he a real, genuine prince? A right down regular, regular, regular royal prince?"

"I don't know about the royalty, but he's a prince in good standing in his own land, and he is also an excellent blacksmith." The Lieutenant chuckled a little. "He and his sister have both been touched a good deal by Tolstoian doctrine. Jack is the most wonderful inventor, I think, that is at present on the earth, Edison notwithstanding. Why, he is just now engaged on a scheme by which he can float houses from the mountains here down to New York. Float them—pipe-line them would perhaps be a better term. You know they have pipe-lines to carry petroleum. Very well; Jack has a solution that dissolves stone as white sugar dissolves in tea, and he believes he can run the fluid from the quarries to where building is going on. It seems that he then puts this liquid into molds, and there you have the stone again. I don't understand the process myself, but Jack tells me it's marvelously cheap, and marvelously effective. He picked up the idea from nature one time when he and I were on our vacation at Detroit."

"Detroit, Michigan?"

"The Detroit River."

"Well, that runs between Michigan and Canada."

"No, no, this is in France. I believe the real name of the river is the Tarn. There's a gorge called Detroit—the strait, you know. Wonderful place—tremendous chasm. You go down in a boat, and all the tributary rivers pour into the main stream like jets from the nozzle of a hose. They tell me this is caused by the rain percolating through the dead leaves on the surface of the ground far above, and thus the water becomes saturated with carbonic acid gas, and so dissolves the limestone until the granite is reached, and the granite forms the bed of these underground rivers. It all seemed to me very wonderful, but it struck Jack on his scientific side, and he has been experimenting ever since. He says he'll be able to build a city with a hose next year."

"Where does he live?"

"On the cruiser just at present. I was instrumental in getting him signed on as John Lamont, and he passed without question. No wonder, for he has scientific degrees from all sorts of German universities, from Oxford, and one or two institutions in the States. When at home he lives in St. Petersburg."

"Has he a palace there?"

Drummond laughed.

"He's got a blacksmith shop, with two rooms above, and I'm going to stop with him for a few months as soon as I get my leave. When the cruiser reaches England we pay off, and I expect to have nothing to do for six months, so Jack and I will make for St. Petersburg."

"Why do you call him Lamont? Is it taken from his real name of what-d'ye-call-it-off?"

"Lermontoff? Yes. The Czar Demetrius, some time about the beginning of the seventeenth century, established a Scottish Guard, just as Louis XI did in France two hundred years before, and there came over from Scotland Lamonts, Carmichaels, Buchanans and others, on whom were bestowed titles and estates. Prince Ivan Lermontoff is a descendant of the original Lamont, who was an officer in the Scottish Guard of Russia.

"So he is really a Scotchman?"

"That's what I tell him when he annoys me, as I am by way of being a Scotchman myself. Ah, the waltz is ended. Will you excuse me a moment while I fetch his Highness?"

Dorothy inclined her head, and Katherine fairly beamed permission.

"Oh, Dorothy," she exclaimed, when the Lieutenant was out of hearing, "think of it! A real prince, and my ambition has never risen higher than a paltry count, or some plebeian of that sort. He's mine, Dorothy; I found him first."

"I thought you had appropriated the Lieutenant?"

"What are lieutenants to me? The proud daughter of a captain (retired) cannot stoop to a mere lieutenant."

"You wouldn't have to stoop far, Kate, with so tall a man as Mr. Drummond."

"You are beginning to take notice, aren't you, Dot? But I bestow the Lieutenant freely upon you, because I'm going to dance with the Prince, even if I have to ask him myself.

> *She'll toddle away, as all aver,*
>
> *With the Lord High Executioner.*

Ah, here they come. Isn't he perfectly splendid? Look at his beard! Just the color of a brand-new twenty-dollar gold piece. See that broad ribbon diagonally across him. I wonder what it means. And gaze at those scintillating orders on his breast. Good gracious me, isn't he splendid?"

"Yes, for a blacksmith. I wonder if he beat those stars out on his anvil. He isn't nearly so tall as Lieutenant Drummond."

"Dorothy, I'll not allow you to disparage my Prince. How can you be so disagreeable? I thought from the very first that the Lieutenant was too tall. If the Prince expects me to call him 'your Highness,' he'll be disappointed."

"You are quite right, Kate. The term would suit the Lieutenant better."

"Dorothy, I believe you're jealous."

"Oh, no, I'm not," said Dorothy, shaking her head and laughing, and then "Hush!" she added, as Katherine was about to speak again.

The next moment the young men stood before them, and, introductions being soberly performed, the Prince lost no time in begging Katherine to favor him with a dance, to which request the young woman was graciously pleased to accede, without, however, exhibiting too much haste about her acceptance, and so they walked off together.

# CHAPTER IV —"AT LAST ALONE"

"SOME one has taken the camp stool," said Lieutenant Drummond. "May I sit here?" and the young woman was good enough to give the desired permission.

When he had seated himself he glanced around, then impulsively held out his hand.

"Miss Amhurst," he said, "how are you?"

"Very well, thank you," replied the girl with a smile, and after half a moment's hesitation she placed her hand in his.

"Of course you dance, Miss Amhurst?"

"Yes, but not to-night. I am here merely as a looker-on in Vienna. You must not allow politeness to keep you away from the floor, or, perhaps, I should say the deck. I don't mind being alone in the least."

"Now, Miss Amhurst, that is not a hint, is it? Tell me that I have not already tired you of my company."

"Oh, no, but I do not wish you to feel that simply because we met casually the other day you are compelled to waste your evening sitting out."

"Indeed, Miss Amhurst, although I should very much like to have the pleasure of dancing with you, there is no one else here that I should care to ask. I have quailed under the eagle eye of my Captain once or twice this evening, and I have been rather endeavoring to keep out of his sight. I fear he has found something new about me of which to disapprove, so I have quite determined not to dance, unless you would consent to dance with me, in which case I am quite ready to brave his reproachful glances."

"Have you done anything wrong lately?"

"Heaven only knows! I try not to be purposely wicked, and indeed have put forth extra efforts to be extra good, but it seems all of no avail. I endeavor to go about the ship with a subdued, humble, unobtrusive air, but this is rather difficult for a person of my size. I don't think a man can droop successfully unless he's under six feet in height."

Dorothy laughed with quiet content. She was surprised to find herself so much at her ease with him, and so mildly happy. They shared a secret together, and that of itself was an intangible bond linking him with her who had no ties with any one else. She liked him; had liked him from the first; and his unconcealed delight in her company was gratifying to a girl who heretofore had found none to offer her the gentle courtesies of life.

"Is it the Russian business again? You do not look very much troubled about it."

"Ah, that is—that is—" he stammered in apparent confusion, then blurted out, "because you—because I am sitting here. Although I have met you but once before, it seems somehow as if I had known you always, and my slight anxiety that I told you of fades away in your presence. I hope you don't think I am forward in saying this, but really to-night, when I saw you at the head of the gangway, I could scarcely refrain from going directly to you and greeting you. I am afraid I made rather a hash of it with Captain Kempt. He is too much of a gentleman to have shown any surprise at my somewhat boisterous accosting of him, and you know I didn't remember him at all, but I saw that you were under his care, and chanced it. Luckily it seems to have been Captain Kempt after all, but I fear I surprised him, taking him by storm, as it were."

"I thought you did it very nicely," said Dorothy, "and, indeed, until this moment I hadn't the least suspicion that you didn't recognize him. He is a dear old gentleman, and I'm very fond of him."

"I say," said the Lieutenant, lowering his voice, "I nearly came a cropper when I spoke of that Russian affair before your friend. I was thinking of—of—well, I wasn't thinking of Miss Kempt—"

"Oh, she never noticed anything," said Dorothy hurriedly. "You got out of that, too, very well. I thought of telling her I had met you before while she and I were in New York together, but the opportunity never seemed—well, I couldn't quite explain, and, indeed, didn't wish to explain my own inexplicable conduct at the bank, and so trusted to chance. If you had greeted me first tonight, I suppose"—she smiled and looked up at him—"I suppose I should have brazened it out somehow."

"Have you been in New York?"

"Yes, we were there nearly a week."

"Ah, that accounts for it."

"Accounts for what?"

"I have walked up and down every street, lane and alley in Bar Harbor, hoping to catch a glimpse of you. I have haunted the town, and all the time you were away."

"No wonder the Captain frowns at you! Have you been neglecting your duty?"

"Well, I have been stretching my shore leave just a little bit. I wanted to apologize for talking so much about myself as we walked from the bank."

"It was very interesting, and, if you remember, we walked farther than I had intended."

"Were your friends waiting for you, or had they gone?"

"They were waiting for me."

"I hope they weren't cross?"

"Oh, no. I told them I had been detained. It happened not to be necessary to enter into details, so I was saved the task of explanation, and, besides, we had other interesting things to discuss. This function on the cruiser has loomed so large as a topic of conversation that there has been little need of any other subject to talk about for several days past."

"I suppose you must have attended many grander occasions than this. Although we have endeavored to make a display, and although we possess a reasonably efficient band, still, a cruiser is not exactly designed for the use to which it is being put to-night. We have many disadvantages to overcome which are not met with in the sumptuous dwellings of New York and Bar Harbor."

The girl's eyes were on the deck for some moments before she replied, then she looked across at the dancers, and finally said:

"I think the ball on the 'Consternation' quite equals anything I have ever attended."

"It is nice of you to say that. Praise from—I won't name Sir Hubert Stanley—but rather Lady Hubert Stanley—is praise, indeed. And now, Miss Amhurst, since I have confessed my fruitless wanderings through Bar Harbor, may I not have the pleasure of calling upon you to-morrow or next day?"

Her eyes were dreamily watching the dancers.

"I suppose," she said slowly, with the flicker of a smile curving those enticing lips, "that since you were so very friendly with Captain Kempt to-night he may expect you to smoke a cigar with him, and it will possibly happen that Katherine and I, who are very fond of the Captain, may chance to come in while you are there."

"Katherine? Ah, Katherine is the name of the young lady who was with you here—Miss Kempt?"

"Yes."

"You are stopping with the Kempts, then?"

"Yes."

"I wonder if they'd think I was taking a liberty if I brought Jack Lamont with me?"

"The Prince?" laughed Dorothy. "Is he a real prince?"

"Oh, yes, there's no doubt about that. I shouldn't have taken the liberty of introducing him to you as Prince Lermontoff if he were not, as we say in

Scotland, a real Mackay—the genuine article. Well, then, the Prince and I will pay our respects to Captain Kempt to-morrow afternoon."

"Did you say the Prince is going with you to Russia?"

"Oh, yes. As I told you, I intend to live very quietly in St. Petersburg, and the Prince has his shop and a pair of rooms above it in a working quarter of the city. I shall occupy one of the rooms and he the other. The Prince is an excellent cook, so we shan't starve, even if we engage no servant."

"Has the Prince given his estates away also?"

"He hasn't given them away exactly, but he is a very indulgent landlord, and he spends so much money on his experiments and travel that, although he has a formidable income, he is very frequently quite short of money. Did you like him?"

"Yes. Of course I saw him for a moment only. I wonder why they haven't returned. There's been several dances since they left."

"Perhaps," said the Lieutenant, with a slight return of his stammering, "your friend may be as fond of dancing as Jack is."

"You are still determined to go to Russia?"

"Quite. There is absolutely no danger. I may not accomplish anything, but I'll have a try at it. The Prince has a good deal of influence in St. Petersburg, which he will use quietly on my behalf, so that I may see the important people. I shall be glad when the Captain ceases frowning—"

Drummond was interrupted by a fellow-officer, who raised his cap, and begged a word with him.

"I think, Drummond, the Captain wanted to see you."

"Oh, did he say that?"

"No, but I know he has left a note for you in your cabin. Shall I go and fetch it?"

"I wish you would, Chesham, if you don't mind, and it isn't too much

54

trouble."

"No trouble at all. Delighted, I'm sure," said Chesham, again raising his cap and going off.

"Now, I wonder what I have forgotten to do."

Drummond heaved a sigh proportionate to himself.

"Under the present condition of things a bit of neglect that would go unnoticed with another man is a sign of unrepentant villainy in me. Any other Lieutenant may steal a horse while I may not look over a hedge. You see how necessary it is for me to go to Russia, and get this thing smoothed over."

"I think, perhaps, you are too sensitive, and notice slights where nothing of the kind is meant," said the girl.

Chesham returned and handed Drummond a letter.

"Will you excuse me a moment?" he said, and as she looked at him he flattered himself that he noticed a trace of anxiety in her eyes. He tore open the missive.

"By Jove!" he cried.

"What is it?" she could not prevent herself from saying, leaning forward.

"I am ordered home. The Admiralty commands me to take the first steamer for England."

"Is that serious?"

He laughed with well-feigned hilarity.

"Oh, no, not serious; it's just their way of doing things. They might easily have allowed me to come home in my own ship. My only fear is I shall have to take the train for New York early to-morrow morning. But," he said, holding out his hands, "it is not serious if you allow me to write to you, and if you will permit me to hope that I may receive an answer."

She placed her hand in his, this time without hesitation.

"You may write," she said, "and I will reply. I trust it is not serious."

# CHAPTER V — AFTER THE OPERA IS OVER

IN mid-afternoon of the day following the entertainment on board the "Consternation" our two girls were seated opposite one another under the rafters of the sewing room, in the listless, desultory manner of those who have not gone home till morning, till daylight did appear. The dominant note of a summer cottage is the rocking-chair, and there were two in the sewing room, where Katherine and Dorothy swayed gently back and forth as they talked. They sat close to the low, broad window which presented so beautiful a picture of the blue Bay and the white shipping. The huge "Consternation" lay moored with her broadside toward the town, all sign of festivity already removed from hull and rigging, and, to the scarcely slumber-satisfied eyes of the girls, something of the sadness of departure seemed to hang as a haze around the great ship. The girls were not discussing the past, but rather anticipating the future; forecasting it, with long, silent pauses intervening.

"So you will not stay with us? You are determined to turn your wealthy back on the poor Kempt family?" Katherine was saying.

"But I shall return to the Kempt family now and then, if they will let me. I must get away for a time and think. My life has suddenly become all topsy-turvy, and I need to get my bearings, as does a ship that has been through a storm and lost her reckoning."

"'She dunno where she are,' as the song says."

"Exactly: that is the state of things."

"I think it's too bad, Dorothy, that you did not allow us to make public announcement of your good fortune. Just imagine what an ovation you would have had on board the cruiser last night if it had been known that the richest woman in that assemblage was a pretty, shy little creature sitting all by herself, and never indulging in even one dance."

"I shouldn't in the least care for that sort of ovation, Kate, and if every one present were as well pleased with the festivities as I, they must all have enjoyed themselves immensely. I believe my friend Kate did my share of the dancing as well as her own."

"'She danced, and she danced, and she danced them a' din.' I think those are the words of the Scottish song that the Prince quoted. He seems up in Scottish poetry, and does not even resent being called a Scotchman. This energetic person of the song seems to have danced them all to a standstill, as I understood him, for he informs me 'a' means 'all' and 'din' means 'done,' but I told him I'd rather learn Russian than Scotch; it was so much easier, and his Highness was good enough to laugh at that. Didn't the Lieutenant ask you to dance at all?"

"Oh, yes, he did."

"And you refused?"

"I refused."

"I didn't think he had sense enough to ask a girl to dance."

"You are ungrateful, Katherine. Remember he introduced you to the Prince."

"Yes, that's so. I had forgotten. I shall never say anything against him again."

"You like the Prince, then?"

"Of all the crowned heads, emperors, kings, sultans, monarchs of every description, dukes, counts, earls, marquises, whom I have met, and who have pestered my life asking me to share their royal perquisites, I think I may say quite truthfully that I like this Jack Lamont better than any one of them."

"Surely Prince Jack has not offered you his principality already?"

"No, not yet, but with an eye to the future I have persuaded him to give up Tolstoi and read Mark Twain, who is not only equally humorous, but much more sensible than the Russian writer. Jack must not be allowed to give away his estates to the peasants as his silly sister has done. I may need them later on."

"Oh, you've got that far, have you?"

"I have got that far: he hasn't. He doesn't know anything about it, but I'll wake him up when the right time comes. There are many elements of sanity about him. He told me that he intended to give up his estates, but in the first place he had been too busy, and in the second he needed the money. His good sense, however, requires refining, so that he may get rid of the dross. I don't blame him; I blame Tolstoi. For instance, when I asked him if he had patented his liquid city invention, he said he did not wish to make a profit from his discovery, but intended it for the good of humanity at large. Imagine such an idiotic idea as that!"

"I think such views are entirely to his credit," alarmed Dorothy.

"Oh, of course, but the plan is not practicable. If he allows such an invention to slip through his fingers, the Standard Oil people will likely get hold of it, form a monopoly, and then where would humanity at large be? I tell him the right way is to patent it, make all the money he can, and use the cash for benefiting humanity under the direction of some charitable person like myself."

"Did you suggest that to him?"

"I did not intimate who the sensible person was, but I elucidated the principle of the thing."

"Yes, and what did he say?"

"Many things, Dorothy, many things. At one time he became confidential about his possessions in foreign lands. It seems he owns several castles, and when he visits any of them he cannot prevent the moujiks, if that is the proper term for the peasantry over there, from prostrating themselves on the ground as he passes by, beating their foreheads against the earth, and chanting, in choice Russian, the phrase: 'Defer, defer, here comes the Lord High Executioner,' or words to that effect. I told him I didn't see why he should interfere with so picturesque a custom, and he said if I visited one of his castles that these estimable people, at a word from him, would form a corduroy road in the mud with their bodies, so that I might step dry-shod from the carriage to the castle doors, and I stipulated that he should at least spread a bit of stair carpet over the poor wretches before I made my progress across his front yard."

"Well, you did become confidential if you discussed a visit to Russia."

"Yes, didn't we? I suppose you don't approve of my forward conduct?"

"I am sure you acted with the utmost prudence, Kate."

"I didn't lose any time, though, did I?"

"I don't know how much time is required to attain the point of friendship you reached. I am inexperienced. It is true I have read of love at first sight, and I am merely waiting to be told whether or not this is an instance of it."

"Oh, you are very diffident, aren't you, sitting there so bashfully!"

"I may seem timid or bashful, but it's merely sleepiness."

"You're a bit of a humbug, Dorothy."

"Why?"

"I don't know why, but you are. No, it was not a case of love at first sight. It was a case of feminine vengeance. Yes, you may look surprised, but I'm telling the truth. After I walked so proudly off with his high mightiness, we had a most agreeable dance together; then I proposed to return to you, but the young man would not have it so, and for the moment I felt flattered. By and by I became aware, however, that it was not because of my company he avoided your vicinity, but that he was sacrificing himself for his friend."

"What friend?"

"Lieutenant Drummond, of course."

"How was he sacrificing himself for Lieutenant Drummond?"

"I surmise that the tall Lieutenant did not fall a victim to my wiles as I had at first supposed, but, in some unaccountable manner, one can never tell how these things happen; he was most anxious to be left alone with the coy

Miss Dorothy Amhurst, who does not understand how long a time it takes to fall in love at first sight, although she has read of these things, dear, innocent girl. The first villain of the piece has said to the second villain of the piece: 'There's a superfluous young woman over on our bench; I'll introduce you to her. You lure her off to the giddy dance, and keep her away as long as you can, and I'll do as much for you some day.'

"Whereupon Jack Lamont probably swore—I understand that profanity is sometimes distressingly prevalent aboard ship—but nevertheless he allowed the Lieutenant to lead him like a lamb to the slaughter. Well, not being powerful enough to throw him overboard when I realized the state of the case, I did the next best thing. I became cloyingly sweet to him. I smiled upon him: I listened to his farrago of nonsense about the chemical components of his various notable inventions, as if a girl attends a ball to study chemistry! Before half an hour had passed the infant had come to the conclusion that here was the first really sensible woman he had ever met. He soon got to making love to me, as the horrid phrase goes, as if love were a mixture to be compounded of this ingredient and that, and then shaken before taken. I am delighted to add, as a testimony to my own powers of pleasing, that Jack soon forgot he was a sacrifice, and really, with a little instruction, he would become a most admirable flirt. He is coming to call upon me this afternoon, and then he will get his eyes opened. I shall tread on him as if he were one of his own moujiks."

"What a wonderful imagination you have, Kate. All you have said is pure fancy. I saw he was taken with you from the very first. He never even glanced at me."

"Of course not: he wasn't allowed to."

"Nonsense, Kate. If I thought for a moment you were really in earnest, I should say you underestimate your own attractions."

"Oh, that's all very well, Miss Dorothy Dimple; you are trying to draw a red herring across the trail, because you know that what I want to hear is why Lieutenant Drummond was so anxious to get me somewhere else. What use did he make of the opportunity the good-natured Prince and my sweet complacency afforded him?"

"He said nothing which might not have been overheard by any one."

"Come down to particulars, Dorothy, and let me judge. You are so inexperienced, you know, that it is well to take counsel with a more sophisticated friend."

"I don't just remember—"

"No, I thought you wouldn't. Did he talk of himself or of you?"

"Of himself, of course. He told me why he was going to Russia, and spoke of some checks he had met in his profession."

"Ah! Did he cash them?"

"Obstacles—difficulties that were in his way, which he hoped to overcome."

"Oh, I see. And did you extend that sympathy which—"

There was a knock at the door, and the maid came in, bearing a card.

"Good gracious me!" cried Katherine, jumping to her feet. "The Prince has come. What a stupid thing that we have no mirror in this room, and it's a sewing and sitting room, too. Do I look all right, Dorothy?"

"To me you seem perfection."

"Ah, well, I can glance at a glass on the next floor. Won't you come down and see him trampled on?"

"No, thank you. I shall most likely drop off to sleep, and enjoy forty winks in this very comfortable chair. Don't be too harsh with the young man, Kate. You are quite wrong in your surmises about him. The Lieutenant never made any such arrangement as you suggest, because he talked of nothing but the most commonplace subjects all the time I was with him, as I was just about to tell you, only you seem in such a hurry to get away."

"Oh, that doesn't deceive me in the least. I'll be back shortly, with the young man's scalp dangling at my belt. Now we shan't be long," and with that Katherine went skipping downstairs.

Dorothy picked up a magazine that lay on the table, and for a few moments turned its leaves from one story to another, trying to interest herself, but failing. Then she lifted the newspaper that lay at her feet, but it also was soon cast aside, and she leaned back in her chair with half-closed eyes, looking out at the cruiser in the Bay. A slight haze arose between her and the ship, thickening and thickening until at last it obscured the vessel.

Dorothy was oppressed by a sense of something forgotten, and she strove in vain to remember what it was. It was of the utmost importance, she was certain, and this knowledge made her mental anxiety the greater.

At last out of the gloom she saw Sabina approach, clothed in rags, and then a flash of intuition enabled her to grasp the difficulty. Through her remissness the ball dress was unfinished, and the girl, springing to her feet, turned intuitively to the sewing-machine, when the ringing laugh of Katherine dissolved the fog.

"Why, you poor girl, what's the matter with you? Are you sitting down to drudgery again? You've forgotten the fortune!"

"Are—are you back already?" cried Dorothy, somewhat wildly.

"Already! Why, bless me, I've been away an hour and a quarter. You dear girl, you've been asleep and in slavery again!"

"I think I was," admitted Dorothy with a sigh.

# CHAPTER VI —FROM SEA TO MOUNTAIN

THREE days later the North Atlantic squadron of the British Navy sailed down the coast from Halifax, did not even pause at Bar Harbor, but sent a wireless telegram to the "Consternation," which pulled up anchor and joined the fleet outside, and so the war-ships departed for another port.

Katherine stood by the broad window in the sewing room in her favorite attitude, her head sideways against the pane, her eyes languidly gazing upon the Bay, fingers drumming this time a very slow march on the window sill. Dorothy sat in a rocking-chair, reading a letter for the second time. There had been silence in the room for some minutes, accentuated rather than broken by the quiet drumming of the girl's fingers on the window sill. Finally Katherine breathed a deep sigh and murmured to herself:

> *"Far called our Navy fades away,*
>
> *On dune and headland sinks the fire.*
>
> *Lo, all our pomp of yesterday*
>
> *Is one with Nineveh and Tyre.'*

I wonder if I've got the lines right," she whispered to herself. She had forgotten there was anyone else in the room, and was quite startled when Dorothy spoke.

"Kate, that's a solemn change, from Gilbert to Kipling. I always judge your mood by your quotations. Has life suddenly become too serious for 'Pinafore' or the 'Mikado'?"

"Oh, I don't know," said Katherine, without turning round. "They are humorous all, and so each furnishes something suitable for the saddened mind. Wisdom comes through understanding your alphabet properly. For instance, first there was Gilbert, and that gave us G; then came Kipling, and he gave us K; thus we get an algebraic formula, G.K., which are the initials of Chesterton, a still later arrival, and as the mind increases in despondency it sinks lower and lower down the alphabet until it comes to S, and thus we have Barn-yard Shaw, an improvement on the Kail-yard school, who takes the O pshaw view of life. And relaxing hold of him I sink deeper until I come to W—W. W. Jacobs—how I wish he wrote poetry! He should be the humorist of all sailors, and perhaps some time he will desert barges for battleships. Then I shall read him with increased enjoyment."

"I wouldn't give Mark Twain for the lot," commented Dorothy with decision.

"Mark Twain isn't yours to give, my dear. He belongs to me also. You've forgotten that comparisons are odious. Our metier is not to compare, but to take what pleases us from each.

'How doth the little busy bee

Improve each shining hour,

And gather honey all the day

From every opening flower.

Watts. You see, I'm still down among the W's. Oh, Dorothy, how can you sit there so placidly when the 'Consternation' has just faded from sight? Selfish creature!

'Oh, give me tears for others' woes

And patience for mine own.'

I don't know who wrote that, but you have no tears for others' woes, merely greeting them with ribald laughter," for Dorothy, with the well-read letter in her hand, was making the rafters ring with her merriment, something that had never before happened during her long tenancy of that room. Kate turned her head slowly round, and the expression on her face was half-indignant, half-humorous, while her eyes were uncertain weather prophets, and gave equal indication of sunshine or rain."

"Why, Katherine, you look like a tragedy queen, rather than the spirit of comedy! Is it really a case of 'Tit-willow, tit-willow, tit-willow'? You see,

I'm a-rescuing you from the bottom of the alphabet, and bringing you up to the Gilbert plane, where I am more accustomed to you, and understand you better. Is this despondency due to the departure of the 'Consternation,' and the fact that she carries away with her Jack Lamont, blacksmith?"

The long sigh terminated in a woeful "yes."

"The ship that has gone out with him we call she. If he had eloped with a real she, then wearing the willow, or singing it, however futile, might be understandable. As it is I see nothing in the situation to call for a sigh."

"That is because you are a hardened sinner, Dorothy. You have no heart, or at least if you have, it is untouched, and therefore you cannot understand. If that note in your hand were a love missive, instead of a letter from your lawyers, you would be more human, Dorothy."

The hand which held the paper crumpled it up slightly as Katherine spoke.

"Business letters are quite necessary, and belong to the world we live in," said Dorothy, a glow of brighter color suffusing her cheeks. "Surely your acquaintance with Mr. Lamont is of the shortest."

"He has called upon me every day since the night of the ball," maintained Katherine stoutly.

"Well, that's only three times."

"Only three! How you talk! One would think you had never been schooled in mathematics. Why, three is a magic figure. You can do plenty of amazing things with it. Don't you know that three is a numeral of love?"

"I thought two was the number," chimed Dorothy, with heartless mirth.

"Three," said Katherine taking one last look at the empty horizon, then seating herself in front of her friend, "three is a recurring decimal. It goes on and on and on forever, and if you write it for a thousand years you are still as far from the end as when you began. It will carry you round the world and back again, and never diminish. It is the mathematical emblem of the nature of true love."

"Is it so serious as all that, Kate, or are you just fooling again?" asked Dorothy, more soberly than heretofore. "Has he spoken to you?"

"Spoken? He has done nothing but speak, and I have listened—oh, so intently, and with such deep understanding. He has never before met such a woman as I, and has frankly told me so."

"I am very glad he appreciates you, dear."

"Yes, you see, Dorothy, I am really much deeper than the ordinary woman. Who, for instance, could find such a beautiful love simile from a book of arithmetic costing twenty-five cents, as I have unearthed from decimal fractions? With that example in mind how can you doubt that other volumes of college learning reveal to me their inner meaning? John presented to me, as he said good-by, a beautifully bound copy of that celebrated text-book, 'Saunders' Analytical Chemistry,' with particularly tender passages marked in pencil, by his own dear hand."

Rather bewildered, for Kate's expression was one of pathos, unrelieved by any gleam of humor, Dorothy nevertheless laughed, although the laugh brought no echo from Katherine.

"And did you give him a volume of Browning in return?"

"No, I didn't. How can you be so unsympathetic? Is it impossible for you to comprehend the unseen link that binds John and me? I rummaged the book store until I found a charming little edition of 'Marshall's Geologist's Pocket Companion,' covered with beautiful brown limp Russia leather—I thought the Russia binding was so inspirational—with a sweet little clasp that keeps it closed—typical of our hands at parting. On the fly-leaf I wrote: 'To J. L., in remembrance of many interesting conversations with his friend, K. K.' It only needed another K to be emblematic and political, a reminiscence of the olden times, when you people of the South, Dorothy, were making it hot for us deserving folks in the North. I hadn't time to go through the book very thoroughly, but I found many references to limestone, which I marked, and one particularly choice bit of English relating to the dissolution and re-

66

consolidation of various minerals I drew a parallelogram around in red ink. A friend of mine in a motor launch was good enough to take the little parcel direct to the 'Consternation,' and I have no doubt that at this moment Jack is perusing it, and perhaps thinking of the giver. I hope it's up-to-date, and that he had not previously bought a copy."

"You don't mean to say, Kate, that your conversation was entirely about geology?"

"Certainly not. How could you have become imbued with an idea so absurd? We had many delightful dalliances down the romantic groves of chemistry, heart-to-heart talks on metallurgy, and once—ah, shall I ever forget it—while the dusk gently enfolded us, and I gazed into those bright, speaking, intelligent eyes of his as he bent nearer and nearer; while his low, sonorous voice in well-chosen words pictured to me the promise which fortified cement holds out to the world; that is, ignorant person, Portland cement strengthened by ribs of steel; and I sat listening breathless as his glowing phrases prophesied the future of this combination."

Katherine closed her eyes, rocked gently back and forth, and crooned, almost inaudibly:

> *"When you gang awa, Jimmie,*
>
> *Faur across the sea, laddie,*
>
> *When ye gang to Russian lands*
>
> *What will ye send to me, laddie?'*

I know what I shall get. It will probably be a newly discovered recipe for the compounding of cement which will do away with the necessity of steel strengthening."

"Kate, dear, you are overdoing it. It is quite right that woman should be a mystery to man, but she should not aspire to become a mystery to her sister woman. Are you just making fun, or is there something in all this more serious than your words imply?"

"Like the steel strengthening in the cement, it may be there, but you can't see it, and you can't touch it, but it makes—oh, such a difference to the slab. Heigho, Dorothy, let us forsake these hard-headed subjects, and turn to something human. What have your lawyers been bothering you about? No trouble over the money, is there?"

Dorothy shook her head.

"No. Of course, there are various matters they have to consult me about, and get my consent to this project or the other."

"Read the letter. Perhaps my mathematical mind can be of assistance to you."

Dorothy had concealed the letter, and did not now produce it.

"It is with reference to your assistance, and your continued assistance, that I wish to speak to you. Let us follow the example of the cement and the steel, and form a compact. In one respect I am going to imitate the 'Consternation.' I leave Bar Harbor next week."

Katherine sat up in her chair, and her eyes opened wide.

"What's the matter with Bar Harbor?" she asked.

"You can answer that question better than I, Kate. The Kempt family are not visitors, but live here all the year round. What do you think is the matter with Bar Harbor?"

"I confess it's a little dull in the winter time, and in all seasons it is situated a considerable distance from New York. Where do you intend to go, Dorothy?"

"That will depend largely on where my friend Kate advises me to go, because I shall take her with me if she will come."

"Companion, lady's-maid, parlor maid, maid-of-all-work, cook, governess, typewriter-girl—which have I to be? Shall I get one afternoon a week off, and may my young man come and see me, if I happen to secure one, and, extremely important, what are the wages?"

"You shall fix your own salary, Kate, and my lawyer men will arrange that the chosen sum is settled upon you so that if we fall out we can quarrel on equal terms."

"Oh, I see, it's an adopted daughter I am to be, then?"

"An adopted sister, rather."

"Do you think I am going to take advantage of my friendship with an heiress, and so pension myself off?"

"It is I who am taking the advantage," said Dorothy, "and I beg you to take compassion, rather than advantage, upon a lone creature who has no kith or kin in the world."

"Do you really mean it, Dot?"

"Of course I do. Should I propose it if I didn't?"

"Well, this is the first proposal I've ever had, and I believe it is customary to say on those occasions that it is so sudden, or so unexpected, and time is required for consideration."

"How soon can you make up your mind, Kate?"

"Oh, my mind's already made up. I'm going to jump at your offer, but I think it more ladylike to pretend a mild reluctance. What are you going to do, Dorothy?"

"I don't know. I've settled on only one thing. I intend to build a little stone and tile church, very quaint and old-fashioned, if I get the right kind of architect to draw a plan for it, and this church is to be situated in Haverstock."

"Where's Haverstock?"

"It is a village near the Hudson River, on the plain that stretches toward the Catskills."

"It was there you lived with your father, was it not?"

"Yes, and my church is to be called the Dr. Amhurst Memorial Church."

"And do you propose to live at Haverstock?"

"I was thinking of that."

"Wouldn't it be just a little dull?"

"Yes, I suppose it is, but it seems to me a suitable place where two young women may meditate on what they are going to do with their lives."

"Yes, that's an important question for the two. I say, Dorothy, let's take the other side of the river, and enter Vassar College. Then we should at least have some fun, and there would be some reasonably well-educated people to speak to."

"Oh, you wish to use your lately acquired scientific knowledge in order to pass the examinations; but, you see, I have had no tutor to school me in the mysteries of lime-burning and the mixing of cement. Now, you have scorned my side of the river, and I have objected to your side of the river. That is the bad beginning which, let us hope, makes the good ending. Who is to arbitrate on our dispute?"

"Why, we'll split the difference, of course."

"How can we do that? Live in a house-boat on the river like Frank Stockton's 'Budder Grange'?"

"No, settle in the city of New York, which is practically an island in the Hudson."

"Would you like to live in New York?"

"Wouldn't I! Imagine any one, having the chance, living anywhere else!"

"In a hotel, I suppose—the Holldorf for choice."

"Yes, we could live in a hotel until we found the ideal flat, high up in a nice apartment house, with a view like that from the top of Mount Washington, or from the top of the Washington Monument."

"But you forget I made one proviso in the beginning, and that is that I am going to build a church, and the church is to be situated, not in the city of New York, but in the village of Haverstock."

"New York is just the place from which to construct such an edifice. Haverstock will be somewhere near the West Shore Railway. Very well. We can take a trip up there once a week or oftener, if you like, and see how the work is progressing, then the people of Haverstock will respect us. As we drive from the station they'll say:

"'There's the two young ladies from New York who are building the church.' But if we settle down amongst them they'll think we're only ordinary villagers instead of the distinguished persons we are. Or, while our flat is being made ready we could live at one of the big hotels in the Catskills, and come down as often as we like on the inclined railway. Indeed, until the weather gets colder, the Catskills is the place.

*And lo, the Catskills print the distant sky,*

*And o'er their airy tops the faint clouds driven,*

*So softly blending that the cheated eye*

*Forgets or which is earth, or which is heaven.'"*

"That ought to carry the day for the Catskills, Kate. What sort of habitation shall we choose? A big hotel, or a select private boarding house?"

"Oh, a big hotel, of course—the biggest there is, whatever its name may be. One of those whose rates are so high that the proprietor daren't advertise them, but says in his announcement, 'for terms apply to the manager.' It must have ample grounds, support an excellent band, and advertise a renowned cuisine. Your room, at least, should have a private balcony on which you can place a telescope and watch the building of your church down below. I, being a humble person in a subordinate position, should have a balcony also to make up for those deficiencies."

"Very well, Kate, that's settled. But although two lone women may set up housekeeping in a New York flat, they cannot very well go alone to a fashionable hotel."

"Oh, yes, we can. Best of references given and required."

"I was going to suggest," pursued Dorothy, not noticing the interruption, "that we invite your father and mother to accompany us. They might enjoy a change from sea air to mountain air."

Katherine frowned a little, and demurred.

"Are you going to be fearfully conventional, Dorothy?"

"We must pay some attention to the conventions, don't you think?"

"I had hoped not. I yearn to be a bachelor girl, and own a latch-key."

"We shall each possess a latch-key when we settle down in New York. Our flat will be our castle, and, although our latch-key will let us in, our Yale lock will keep other people out. A noted summer resort calls for different treatment, because there we lead a semi-public life. Besides, I am selfish enough to wish my coming-out to be under the auspices of so well-known a man as Captain Kempt."

"All right, I'll see what they say about it. You don't want Sabina, I take it?"

"Yes, if she will consent to come."

"I doubt if she will, but I'll see. Besides, now that I come to think about it, it's only fair I should allow my doting parents to know that I am about to desert them."

With that Katherine quitted the room, and went down the stairs hippety-hop.

Dorothy drew the letter from its place of concealment, and read it for the third time, although one not interested might have termed it a most commonplace document. It began:

"Dear Miss Amhurst," and ended "Yours most sincerely, Alan Drummond." It gave some account of his doings since he bade good-bye to her. A sailor, he informed her, needs little time for packing his belongings, and on the occasion in question the Prince had been of great assistance. They set out together for the early morning train, and said "au revoir" at the station. Drummond had intended to sail from New York, but a friendly person whom he met on the train informed him that the Liverpool liner "Enthusiana" set out from Boston next day, so he had abandoned the New York idea, and had taken passage on the liner named, on whose note-paper he wrote the letter, which epistle was once more concealed as Dorothy heard Katherine's light step on the stair.

That impulsive young woman burst into the sewing room.

"We're all going," she cried. "Father, mother and Sabina. It seems father has had an excellent offer to let the house furnished till the end of September, and he says that, as he likes high life, he will put in the time on the top of the Catskills. He abandons me, and says that if he can borrow a shilling he is going to cut me off with it in his will. He regrets the departure of the British Fleet, because he thinks he might have been able to raise a real English shilling aboard. Dad only insists on one condition, namely, that he is to pay for himself, mother and Sabina, so he does not want a room with a balcony. I said that in spite of his disinheritance I'd help the family out of my salary, and so he is going to reconsider the changing of his will."

"We will settle the conditions when we reach the Catskills," said Dorothy, smiling.

# CHAPTER VII —"A WAY THEY HAVE IN THE NAVY"

CAPTAIN and Mrs. Kempt with Sabina had resided a week in the Matterhorn Hotel before the two girls arrived there. They had gone direct to New York, and it required the seven days to find a flat that suited them, of which they were to take possession on the first of October. Then there were the lawyers to see; a great many business details to settle, and an architect to consult. After leaving New York the girls spent a day at Haverstock, where Dorothy Amhurst bought a piece of land as shrewdly as if she had been in the real estate business all her life. After this transaction the girls drove to the station on the line connecting with the inclined railway, and so, as Katherine remarked, were "wafted to the skies on flowery beds of ease," which she explained to her shocked companion was all right, because it was a quotation from a hymn. When at last they reached their hotel, Katherine was in ecstasies.

"Isn't this heavenly?" she cried, "and, indeed, it ought to be, for I understand we are three thousand feet higher than we were in New York, and even the sky-scrapers can't compete with such an altitude."

The broad valley of the Hudson lay spread beneath them, stretching as far as the eye could see, shimmering in the thin, bluish veil of a summer evening, and miles away the river itself could be traced like a silver ribbon.

The gallant Captain, who had been energetically browbeaten by his younger daughter, and threatened with divers pains and penalties should he fail to pay attention and take heed to instructions, had acquitted himself with eclat in the selection of rooms for Dorothy and his daughter. The suite was situated in one corner of the huge caravansary, a large parlor occupying the angle, with windows on one side looking into the forest, and on the other giving an extended view across the valley. The front room adjoining the parlor was to be Dorothy's very own, and the end room belonged to Katherine, he said, as long as she behaved herself. If Dorothy ever wished to evict her strenuous neighbor, all she had to do was to call upon the Captain, and he would lend his aid, at which proffer of assistance Katherine tossed her head, and said she would try the room for a week, and, if she didn't like it, out Dorothy would have to go.

There followed days and nights of revelry. Hops, concerts, entertainments of all sorts, with a more pretentious ball on Saturday night, when the week-tired man from New York arrived in the afternoon to find temperature twenty degrees lower, and the altitude very much higher than was the case in his busy office in the city. Katherine revelled in this round of excitement, and indeed, so, in a milder way, did Dorothy. After the functions were over the girls enjoyed a comforting chat with one another in their drawing room; all windows open, and the moon a-shining down over the luminous valley, which it seemed to fill with mother-o'-pearl dust.

Young Mr. J. K. Henderson of New York, having danced repeatedly with Katherine on Saturday night, unexpectedly turned up for the hop on the following Wednesday, when he again danced repeatedly with the same joyous girl. It being somewhat unusual for a keen business man to take a four hours' journey during an afternoon in the middle of the week, and, as a consequence, arrive late at his office next morning, Dorothy began to wonder if a concrete formation, associated with the name of Prince Ivan Lermontoff of Russia, was strong enough to stand an energetic assault of this nature, supposing it were to be constantly repeated. It was after midnight on Wednesday when the two reached the corner parlor. Dorothy sat in a cane armchair, while Katherine threw herself into a rocking-chair, laced her fingers behind her head, and gazed through the open window at the misty infinity beyond.

"Well," sighed Katherine, "this has been the most enjoyable evening I ever spent!"

"Are you quite sure?" inquired her friend.

"Certainly. Shouldn't I know?"

"He dances well, then?"

"Exquisitely!"

"Better than Jack Lamont?"

"Well, now you mention him I must confess Jack danced very creditably."

"I didn't know but you might have forgotten the Prince."

"No, I haven't exactly forgotten him, but—I do think he might have written to me."

"Oh, that's it, is it? Did he ask your permission to write?"

"Good gracious, no. We never talked of writing. Old red sandstone, rather, was our topic of conversation. Still, he might have acknowledged receipt of the book."

"But the book was given to him in return for the one he presented to you."

"Yes, I suppose it was. I hadn't thought of that."

"Then again, Kate, Russian notions regarding writing to young ladies may differ from ours, or he may have fallen overboard, or touched a live wire."

"Yes, there are many possibilities," murmured Katherine dreamily.

"It seems rather strange that Mr. Henderson should have time to come up here in the middle of the week."

"Why is it strange?" asked Katherine. "Mr. Henderson is not a clerk bound down to office hours. He's an official high up in one of the big insurance companies, and gets a simply tremendous salary."

"Really? Does he talk as well as Jack Lamont did?"

"He talks less like the Troy Technical Institute, and more like the 'Home Journal' than poor Prince Jack did, and then he has a much greater sense of humor. When I told him that the oath of an insurance man should be 'bet your life!' he laughed. Now, Jack would never have seen the point of that. Anyhow, the hour is too late, and I am too sleepy, to worry about young men, or jokes either. Good-night!"

Next morning's mail brought Dorothy a bulky letter decorated with English stamps. She locked the door, tore open the envelope, and found many sheets of thin paper bearing the heading of the Bluewater Club, Pall Mall.

"I am reminded of an old adage," she read, "to the effect that one should never cross a bridge before arriving at it. Since I bade good-by to you, up to this very evening, I have been plodding over a bridge that didn't exist, much to my own discomfort. You were with me when I received the message ordering me home to England, and I don't know whether or not I succeeded in suppressing all signs of my own perturbation, but we have in the Navy now a man who does not hesitate to overturn a court martial, and so I feared a re-opening of the Rock in the Baltic question, which might have meant the wrecking of my career. I had quite made up my mind, if the worst came to the worst, to go out West and become a cow-boy, but a passenger with whom I became acquainted on the 'Enthusiana' informed me, to my regret, that the cow-boy is largely a being of the past, to be met with only in the writings of Stewart Edward White, Owen Wister, and several other famous men whom he named. So you see, I went across the ocean tolerably depressed, finding my present occupation threatened, and my future uncertain.

"When I arrived in London I took a room at this Club, of which I have been a member for some years, and reported immediately at the Admiralty. But there, in spite of all diligence on my part, I was quite unable to learn what was wanted of me. Of course, I could have gone to my Uncle, who is in the government, and perhaps he might have enlightened me, although he has nothing to do with the Navy, but I rather like to avoid Uncle Metgurne. He brought me up since I was a small boy, and seems unnecessarily ashamed of the result. It is his son who is the attache' in St. Petersburg that I spoke to you about."

Dorothy ceased reading for a moment.

"Metgurne, Metgurne," she said to herself. "Surely I know that name?"

She laid down the letter, pressed the electric button, and unlocked the door. When the servant came, she said:

"Will you ask at the office if they have any biographical book of reference relating to Great Britain, and if so, please bring it to me."

The servant appeared shortly after with a red book which proved to be an English "Who's Who" dated two years back. Turning the pages she came to Metgurne.

"Metgurne, twelfth Duke of, created 1681, Herbert George Alan." Here followed a number of other titles, the information that the son and heir was Marquis of Thaxted, and belonged to the Diplomatic Service, that Lord Metgurne was H. M. Secretary of State for Royal Dependencies; finally a list of residences and clubs. She put down the book and resumed the letter.

"I think I ought to have told you that when I reach St. Petersburg I shall be as anxious to avoid my cousin Thaxted as I am to steer clear of his father in London. So I sat in my club, and read the papers. Dear me, this is evidently going to be a very long letter. I hope you won't mind. I think perhaps you may be interested in learning how they do things over here.

"After two or three days of anxious waiting there came a crushing communication from the Admiralty which confirmed my worst fears and set me at crossing the bridge again. I was ordered to report next morning at eleven, at Committee Room 5, in the Admiralty, and bring with me full particulars pertaining to the firing of gun number so-and-so of the 'Consternation's' equipment on such a date. I wonder since that I did not take to drink. We have every facility for that sort of thing in this club. However, at eleven next day, I presented myself at the Committee Room and found in session the grimmest looking five men I have ever yet been called upon to face. Collectively they were about ten times worse in appearance than the court-martial I had previously encountered. Four of the men I did not know, but the fifth I recognized at once, having often seen his portrait. He is Admiral Sir John Pendergest, popularly known in the service as 'Old Grouch,' a blue terror who knows absolutely nothing of mercy. The lads in the service say he looks so disagreeable because he is sorry he wasn't born a hanging judge. Picture a face as cleanly cut as that of some severe old Roman Senator; a face as hard as marble, quite as cold, and nearly as white, rescued from the appearance of a death mask by a pair of piercing eyes that glitter like steel. When looking at him it is quite impossible to believe that such a personage has ever been a boy who played pranks on his masters. Indeed, Admiral Sir John Pendergest seems to have sprung, fully uniformed and forbidding, from the earth, like those soldiers of mythology. I was so taken aback at confronting such a man that I never noticed my old friend, Billy Richardson, seated at the table as one of the minor officials of the Committee. Billy tells me I looked rather white about the lips when I realized what was ahead of me, and I daresay he was right. My consolation is that I didn't get red, as is my disconcerting habit. I was accommodated with a chair, and then a ferrety-faced little man began asking me questions, consulting every now and then a foolscap sheet of paper which was before him. Others were ready to note down the answers.

"'When did you fire the new gun from the "Consternation" in the Baltic?'

"Dear Miss Amhurst, I have confessed to you that I am not brilliant, and, indeed, such confession was quite unnecessary, for you must speedily have recognized the fact, but here let me boast for a line or two of my one accomplishment, which is mathematical accuracy. When I make experiments I don't note the result by rule of thumb. My answer to the ferret-faced man was prompt and complete.

"'At twenty-three minutes, seventeen seconds past ten, A.M., on May the third of this year,' was my reply.

"The five high officials remained perfectly impassive, but the two stenographers seemed somewhat taken by surprise, and one of them whispered, 'Did you say fifteen seconds, sir?'

"'He said seventeen,' growled Sir John Pendergest, in a voice that seemed to come out of a sepulchre.

"'Who sighted the gun?'

"'I did, sir.'

"'Why did not the regular gunner do that?'

"'He did, sir, but I also took observations, and raised the muzzle .000327 of an inch.'

"'Was your gunner inaccurate, then, to that extent?'

"'No, sir, but I had weighed the ammunition, and found it short by two ounces and thirty-seven grains.'

"I must not bore you with all the questions and answers. I merely give these as samples. They questioned me about the recoil, the action of the gun, the state of this, that and the other after firing, and luckily I was able to answer to a dot every query put to me. At the finish one of the judges asked me to give in my own words my opinion of the gun. Admiral Sir John glared at him as he put this question, for of course to any expert the answers I had furnished, all taken together, gave an accurate verdict on the gun, assuming my statements to have been correct, which I maintain they were. However, as Sir John made no verbal comment, I offered my opinion as tersely as I could.

"'Thank you, Lieutenant Drummond,' rumbled Sir John in his deep voice, as if he were pronouncing sentence, and, my testimony completed, the Committee rose.

"I was out in the street before Billy Richardson overtook me, and then he called himself to my attention by a resounding slap on the shoulder.

"'Alan, my boy,' he cried, 'you have done yourself proud. Your fortune's made.'

"'As how?' I asked, shaking him by the hand.

"'Why, we've been for weeks holding an inquiry on this blessed gun, and the question is whether or not a lot more of them are to be made. You know what an opinionated beast Old Grouch is. Well, my boy, you have corroborated his opinion of the gun in every detail. He is such a brow-beating, tyrannical brute that the rest of the Committee would rather like to go against him if they dared, but you have put a spoke in their wheel. Why, Sir John never said "thank you" to a human being since he was born until twenty-seven minutes and fifteen seconds after eleven this morning, as you would have put it,' and at the time of writing this letter this surmise of Billy's appears to be justified, for the tape in the club just now announced that the Committee has unanimously decided in favor of the gun, and adds that this is regarded as a triumph for the chairman, Admiral Sir John Pendergest, with various letters after his name.

"Dear Miss Amhurst, this letter, as I feared, has turned out intolerably long, and like our first conversation, it is all about myself. But then, you see, you are the only one on the other side of the water to whom I have confided my selfish worries, and I believe you to be so kind-hearted that I am sure you will not censure me for this once exceeding the limits of friendly correspondence. Having been deeply depressed during all the previous long days, the sudden reaction urges me to go out into Pall Mall, fling my cap in the air, and whoop, which action is quite evidently a remnant of my former cow-boy aspirations. Truth to tell, the Russian business seems already forgotten, except by my stout old Captain on the 'Consternation,' or my Uncle. The strenuous Sir John has had me haled across the ocean merely to give testimony, lasting about thirty-five minutes, when with a little patience he might have waited till the 'Consternation' herself arrived, or else have cabled for us to try the gun at Bar Harbor. I suppose, however, that after my unfortunate contretemps with Russia our government was afraid I'd chip a corner off the United States, and that they'd have to pay for it. So perhaps after all it was greater economy to bring me across on the liner 'Enthusiana.'

"By the way, I learned yesterday that the 'Consternation' has been ordered home, and so I expect to see Jack Lamont before many days are past. The ship will be paid off at Portsmouth, and then I suppose he and I will have our freedom for six months. I am rather looking forward to Jack's cooking me some weird but tasteful Russian dishes when we reach his blacksmith's shop in St. Petersburg. If I get on in Russia as I hope and expect, I shall spend the rest of my leave over in the States. I saw very little indeed of that great country, and am extremely anxious to see more. When one is on duty aboard ship one can only take very short excursions ashore. I should like to visit Niagara. It seems ridiculous that one should have been all along the American coast from Canada to New York, and never have got far enough inland to view the great Falls.

"Russia is rather dilatory in her methods, but I surely should know within two or three weeks whether I am going to succeed or not. If not, then there is no use in waiting there. I shall try to persuade the Prince to accompany me to

America. During the weeks I am waiting in St. Petersburg I shall continually impress upon him the utter futility of a life which has not investigated the great electrical power plant at Niagara Falls. And then he is interested in the educational system of the United States. While we were going to the station early that morning he told me that the United States educational system must be the most wonderful in the world, because he found that your friend, Miss Katherine Kempt, knew more about electricity, metallurgy, natural philosophy and a great number of other things he is interested in, than all the ladies he has met in Europe put together. He thinks that's the right sort of education for girls, and all this rather astonished me, because, although your friend was most charming, she said nothing during my very short acquaintance with her to lead me to suspect that she had received a scientific training.

"Dear Miss Amhurst, I am looking every day for a letter from you, but none has yet been received by the Admiralty, who, when they get one, will forward it to whatever part of the world I happen to be in."

# CHAPTER VIII —"WHEN JOHNNY COMES MARCHING HOME"

A SUMMER hotel that boasts a thousand acres of forest, more or less, which serve the purposes of a back-yard, affords its guests, even if all its multitude of rooms are occupied, at least one spot for each visitor to regard as his or her favorite nook. So large an extent of woodland successfully defies landscape gardening. It insists on being left alone, and its very immensity raises a financial barrier against trimly-kept gravel walks. There were plenty of landscape garden walks in the immediate vicinity of the hotel, and some of them ambitiously penetrated into the woods, relapsing from the civilization of beaten gravel into a primitive thicket trail, which, however, always led to some celebrated bit of picturesqueness: a waterfall, or a pulpit rock upstanding like a tower, or the fancied resemblance of a human face carved by Nature from the cliff, or a view-point jutting out over the deep chasm of the valley, which usually supported a rustic summer house or pavilion where unknown names were carved on the woodwork—the last resort of the undistinguished to achieve immortality by means of a jack-knife.

Dorothy discovered a little Eden of her own, to which no discernible covert-way led, for it was not conspicuous enough to obtain mention in the little gratis guide which the hotel furnished—a pamphlet on coated paper filled with half-tone engravings, and half-extravagant eulogies of what it proclaimed to be, an earthly paradise, with the rates by the day or week given on the cover page to show on what terms this paradise might be enjoyed.

Dorothy's bower was green, and cool, and crystal, the ruggedness of the rocks softened by the wealth of foliage. A very limpid spring, high up and out of sight among the leaves, sent its waters tinkling down the face of the cliff, ever filling a crystal-clear lakelet at the foot, which yet was never full. Velvety and beautiful as was the moss surrounding this pond, it was nevertheless too damp to form an acceptable couch for a human being, unless that human being were brave enough to risk the rheumatic inconveniences which followed Rip Van Winkle's long sleep in these very regions, so Dorothy always carried with her from the hotel a feather-weight, spider's-web hammock, which she deftly slung between two saplings, their light suppleness giving an almost pneumatic effect to this fairy net spread in a fairy glen; and here the young woman swayed luxuriously in the relaxing delights of an indolence still too new to have become commonplace or wearisome.

She always expected to read a great deal in the hammock, but often the book slipped unnoticed to the moss, and she lay looking upward at the little discs of blue sky visible through the checkering maze of green leaves. One afternoon, deserted by the latest piece of fictional literature, marked in plain figures on the paper cover that protected the cloth binding, one dollar and a half, but sold at the department stores for one dollar and eight cents, Dorothy lay half-hypnotized by the twinkling of the green leaves above her, when she heard a sweet voice singing a rollicking song of the Civil War, and so knew that Katherine was thus heralding her approach.

> *"When Johnny comes marching home again,*
>
> *Hurrah! Hurrah!*
>
> *We'll give him a hearty welcome then,*
>
> *Hurrah! Hurrah!*
>
> *The men will cheer, the boys will shout,*
>
> *The ladies they will all turn out,*
>
> *And we'll all feel gay*
>
> *When Johnny comes marching home.'"*

Dorothy went still further back into the history of her country, and gave a faint imitation of an Indian war-whoop, to let the oncomer know she was welcome, and presently Katherine burst impetuously through the dense undergrowth.

"So here you are, Miss Laziness," she cried.

"Here I am, Miss Energy, or shall I call you Miss-applied Energy?

Katherine, you have walked so fast that you are quite red in the face."

"It isn't exertion, it's vexation. Dorothy, I have had a perfectly terrible time. It is the anxiety regarding the proper discipline of parents that is spoiling the nervous system of American children. Train them up in the way they should go, and when they are old they do depart from it. There's nothing more awful than to own parents who think they possess a sense of humor. Thank goodness mother has none!"

"Then it is your father who has been misbehaving?"

"Of course it is. He treats the most serious problem of a woman's life as if it were the latest thing in 'Life.'"

Dorothy sat up in the hammock.

"The most important problem? That means a proposal. Goodness gracious, Kate, is that insurance man back here again?"

"What insurance man?"

"Oh, heartless and heart-breaking Katherine, is there another? Sit here in the hammock beside me, and tell me all about it."

"No, thank you," refused Katherine. "I weigh more than you, and I cannot risk my neck through the collapse of that bit of gossamer. I must take care of myself for his sake."

"Then it is the life insurance man whose interests you are consulting? Have you taken out a policy with him?"

"Dear me, you are nearly as bad as father, but not quite so funny. You are referring to Mr. Henderson, I presume. A most delightful companion for a dance, but, my dear Dorothy, life is not all glided out to the measures of a Strauss waltz."

"True; quite undisputable, Kate, and them sentiments do you credit. Who is the man?"

"The human soul," continued Katherine seriously, "aspires to higher things than the society columns of the New York Sunday papers, and the frivolous chatter of an overheated ball-room."

"Again you score, Kate, and are rising higher and higher in my estimation. I see it all now. Those solemn utterances of yours point directly toward Hugh Miller's 'Old Red Sandstone' and works of that sort, and now I remember your singing 'When Johnny comes marching home.' I therefore take it that Jack Lamont has arrived."

"He has not."

"Then he has written to you?"

"He has not."

"Oh, well, I give it up. Tell me the tragedy your own way."

For answer Katherine withdrew her hands from behind her, and offered to her friend a sheet of paper she had been holding. Dorothy saw blazoned on the top of it a coat-of-arms, and underneath it, written in words of the most formal nature, was the information that Prince Ivan Lermontoff presented his warmest regards to Captain Kempt, U.S.N., retired, and begged permission to pay his addresses to the Captain's daughter Katherine. Dorothy looked up from the document, and her friend said calmly:

"You see, they need another Katherine in Russia."

"I hope she won't be like a former one, if all I've read of her is true. This letter was sent to your father, then?"

"It was, and he seems to regard it as a huge joke. Said he was going to cable his consent, and as the 'Consternation' has sailed away, he would try to pick her up by wireless telegraphy, and secure the young man that way: suggests that I shall have a lot of new photographs taken, so that he can hand them out to the reporters when they call for particulars. Sees in his mind's eye, he says, a huge black-lettered heading in the evening papers: 'A Russian Prince captures one of our fairest daughters,' and then insultingly hinted that perhaps, after all, it was better not to use my picture, as it might not bear out the 'fair daughter' fiction of the heading."

"Yes, Kate, I can see that such treatment of a vital subject must have been very provoking."

"Provoking? I should say it was! He pretended he was going to tack this letter up on the notice-board in the hall of the hotel, so that every one might know what guests of distinction the Matterhorn House held. But the most exasperating feature of the situation is that this letter has been lying for days and days at our cottage in Bar Harbor. I am quite certain that I left instructions for letters to be forwarded, but, as nothing came, I telegraphed yesterday to the people who have taken our house, and now a whole heap of belated correspondence has arrived, with a note from our tenant saying he did not know our address. You will see at the bottom of the note that the Prince asks my father to communicate with him by sending a reply to the 'Consternation' at New York, but now the 'Consternation' has sailed for England, and poor John must have waited and waited in vain."

"Write care of the 'Consternation' in England."

"But Jack told me that the 'Consternation' paid off as soon as she arrived, and probably he will have gone to Russia."

"If you address him at the Admiralty in London, the letter will be forwarded wherever he happens to be."

"How do you know?"

"I have heard that such is the case."

"But you're not sure, and I want to be certain."

"Are you really in love with him, Kate?"

"Of course I am. You know that very well, and I don't want any stupid misapprehension to arise at the beginning, such as allows a silly author to carry on his story to the four-hundredth page of such trash as this," and she gently touched with her toe the unoffending volume which lay on the ground beneath the hammock.

"Then why not adopt your father's suggestion, and cable? It isn't you who are cabling, you know."

"I couldn't consent to that. It would look as if we were in a hurry, wouldn't it?"

"Then let me cable."

"You? To whom?"

"Hand me up that despised book, Kate, and I'll write my cablegram on the fly-leaf. If you approve of the message, I'll go to the hotel, and send it at once."

Katherine gave her the book, and lent the little silver pencil which hung jingling, with other trinkets, on the chain at her belt. Dorothy scribbled a note, tore out the fly-leaf, and presented it to Katherine, who read:

"Alan Drummond, Bluewater Club, Pall Mall, London. Tell Lamont that his letter to Captain Kempt was delayed, and did not reach the Captain until to-day. Captain Kempt's reply will be sent under cover to you at your club. Arrange for forwarding if you leave England.

"Dorothy Amhurst."

When Katherine finished reading she looked up at her friend, and exclaimed: "Well!" giving that one word a meaning deep as the clear pool on whose borders she stood.

Dorothy's face reddened as if the sinking western sun was shining full upon it.

"You write to one another, then?"

"Yes."

"And is it a case of—"

"No; friendship."

"Sure it is nothing more than that?"

Dorothy shook her head.

"Dorothy, you are a brick; that's what you are. You will do anything to help a friend in trouble."

Dorothy smiled.

"I have so few friends that whatever I can do for them will not greatly tax any capabilities I may possess."

"Nevertheless, Dorothy, I thoroughly appreciate what you have done. You did not wish any one to know you were corresponding with him, and yet you never hesitated a moment when you saw I was anxious."

"Indeed, Kate, there was nothing to conceal. Ours is a very ordinary exchange of letters. I have only had two: one at Bar Harbor a few days after he left, and another longer one since we came to the hotel, written from England."

"Did the last one go to Bar Harbor, too? How came you to receive it when we did not get ours?"

"It did not go to Bar Harbor. I gave him the address of my lawyers in New York, and they forwarded it to me here. Lieutenant Drummond was ordered home by some one who had authority to do so, and received the message while he was sitting with me on the night of the ball. He had got into trouble with Russia. There had been an investigation, and he was acquitted. I saw that he was rather worried over the order home and I expressed my sympathy as well as I could, hoping everything would turn out for the best. He asked if he might write and let me know the outcome, and, being interested, I quite willingly gave him permission, and my address. The letter I received was all about a committee meeting at the Admiralty in which he took part. He wrote to me from the club in Pall Mall to which I have addressed this cablegram."

There was a sly dimple in Katherine's cheeks as she listened to this straightforward explanation, and the faintest possible suspicion of a smile flickered at the corner of her mouth. She murmured, rather than sang:

"'A pair of lovesick maidens we.'"

"One, if you please," interrupted Dorothy.

"'Lovesick all against our will—'"

"Only one."

"'Twenty years hence we shan't be A pair of lovesick maidens still.'"

"I am pleased to note," said Dorothy demurely, "that the letter written by the Prince to your father has brought you back to the Gilbert and Sullivan plane again, although in this fairy glen you should quote from Iolanthe rather than from Patience."

"Yes, Dot, this spot might do for a cove in the 'Pirates of Penzance,' only we're too far from the sea. But, to return to the matter in hand, I don't think there will be any need to send that cablegram. I don't like the idea of a cablegram, anyhow. I will return to the hotel, and dictate to my frivolous father a serious composition quite as stately and formal as that received from the Prince. He will address it and seal it, and then if you are kind enough to enclose it in the next letter you send to Lieutenant Drummond, it will be sure to reach Jack Lamont ultimately."

Dorothy sprang from the hammock to the ground.

"Oh," she cried eagerly, "I'll go into the hotel with you and write my letter at once."

Katherine smiled, took her by the arm, and said:

"You're a dear girl, Dorothy. I'll race you to the hotel, as soon as we are through this thicket."

# CHAPTER IX —IN RUSSIA

THE next letter Dorothy received bore Russian stamps, and was dated at the black-smith's shop, Bolshoi Prospect, St. Petersburg. After a few preliminaries, which need not be set down here, Drummond continued:

"The day after Jack arrived in London, there being nothing whatever to detain him in England, we set off together for St. Petersburg, and are now domiciled above his blacksmith shop. We are not on the fashionable side of the river, but our street is wide, and a very short walk brings us to a bridge which, being crossed, allows us to wander among palaces if we are so disposed. We have been here only four days, yet a good deal has already been accomplished. The influence of the Prince has smoothed my path for me. Yesterday I had an audience with a very important personage in the Foreign Office, and to-day I have seen an officer of high rank in the navy. The Prince warns me to mention no names, because letters, even to a young lady, are sometimes opened before they reach the person to whom they are addressed. These officials who have been kind enough to receive me are gentlemen so polished that I feel quite uncouth in their presence. I am a little shaky in my French, and feared that my knowledge of that language might not carry me through, but both of these officials speak English much better than I do, and they seemed rather pleased I had voluntarily visited St. Petersburg to explain that no discourtesy was meant in the action I had so unfortunately taken on the Baltic, and they gave me their warmest assurances they would do what they could to ease the tension between our respective countries. It seems that my business here will be finished much sooner than I expected, and then I am off on the quickest steamer for New York, in the hope of seeing Niagara Falls. I have met with one disappointment, however. Jack says he cannot possibly accompany me to the United States. I have failed to arouse in him the faintest interest about the electric works at Niagara. He insists that he is on the verge of a most important discovery, the nature of which he does not confide in me. I think he is working too hard, for he is looking quite haggard and overdone, but that is always the way with him. He throws himself heart and soul into any difficulty that confronts him, and works practically night and day until he has solved it.

"Yesterday he gave the whole street a fright. I had just returned from the Foreign Office, and had gone upstairs to my room, when there occurred an explosion that shook the building from cellar to roof, and sent the windows of our blacksmith's shop rattling into the street. Jack had a most narrow escape, but is unhurt, although that fine beard of his was badly singed. He has had it shaved off, and now sports merely a mustache, looking quite like a man from New York. You wouldn't recognize him if you met him on Broadway. The carpenters and glaziers are at work to-day repairing the damage. I told Jack that if this sort of thing kept on I'd be compelled to patronize another hotel, but he says it won't happen again. It seems he was trying to combine two substances by adding a third, and, as I understood him, the mixing took place with unexpected suddenness. He has endeavored to explain to me the reaction, as he calls it, which occurred, but I seem to have no head for chemistry, and besides, if I am to be blown through the roof some of these days it will be no consolation to me when I come down upon the pavement outside to know accurately the different elements which contributed to my elevation. Jack is very patient in trying to instruct me, but he could not resist the temptation of making me ashamed by saying that your friend, Miss Katherine Kempt, would have known at once the full particulars of the reaction. Indeed, he says, she warned him of the disaster, by marking a passage in a book she gave him which foreshadowed this very thing. She must be a most remarkable young woman, and it shows how stupid I am that I did not in the least appreciate this fact when in her company."

The next letter was received a week later. He was getting on swimmingly, both at the Foreign Office and at the Russian Admiralty. All the officials he had met were most courteous and anxious to advance his interests. He wrote about the misapprehensions held in England regarding Russia, and expressed his resolve to do what he could when he returned to remove these false impressions.

"Of course," he went on, "no American or Englishman can support or justify the repressive measures so often carried out ruthlessly by the Russian police. Still, even these may be exaggerated, for the police have to deal with a people very much different from our own. It is rather curious that at this moment I am in vague trouble concerning the police. I am sure this place is watched, and I am also almost certain that my friend Jack is being shadowed. He dresses like a workman; his grimy blouse would delight the heart of his friend Tolstoi, but he is known to be a Prince, and I think the authorities imagine he is playing up to the laboring class, whom they despise. I lay it all to that unfortunate explosion, which gathered the police about us as if they had sprung from the ground. There was an official examination, of course, and Jack explained, apparently to everybody's satisfaction, exactly how he came to make the mistake that resulted in the loss of his beard and his windows. I don't know exactly how to describe the feeling of uneasiness which has come over me. At first sight this city did not strike me as so very much different from New York or London, and meeting, as I did, so many refined gentlemen in high places, I had come to think St. Petersburg was after all very much like Paris, or Berlin, or Rome. But it is different, and the difference makes itself subtly felt, just as the air in some coast towns of Britain is relaxing, and in others bracing. In these towns a man doesn't notice the effect at first, but later on he begins to feel it, and so it is here in St. Petersburg. Great numbers of workmen pass down our street. They all seem to know who the Prince is, and the first days we were here, they saluted him with a deference which I supposed was due to his rank, in spite of the greasy clothes he wore. Since the explosion an indefinable change has come over these workmen. They salute the Prince still when we meet them on the street, but there is in their attitude a certain sly sympathy, if I may so term it; a bond of camaraderie which is implied in their manner rather than expressed. Jack says this is all fancy on my part, but I don't think it is. These men imagine that Prince Ivan Lermontoff, who lives among them and dresses like them, is concocting some explosive which may yet rid them of the tyrants who make their lives so unsafe. All this would not matter, but what does matter is the chemical reaction, as I believe Jack would term it, which has taken place among the authorities. The authorities undoubtedly have their spies among the working-men, and know well what they are thinking about and talking about. I do not believe they were satisfied with the explanations Jack gave regarding the disaster. I have tried to impress upon Jack that he must be more careful in walking about the town, and I have tried to persuade him, after work, to dress like the gentleman he is, but he laughs at my fears, and assures me that I have gone from one extreme to the other in my opinion of St. Petersburg. First I thought it was like all other capitals; now I have swung too far in the other direction. He says the police of St. Petersburg would not dare arrest him, but I'm not so sure of that. A number of things occur to me, as usual, too late. Russia, with her perfect secret service system, must know that Prince Lermontoff has been serving in the British Navy. They know he returned to St. Petersburg, avoids all his old friends, and is brought to their notice by an inexplicable explosion, and they must be well aware, also, that he is in the company of the man who fired the shell at the rock in the Baltic, and that he himself served on the offending cruiser.

"As to my own affairs, I must say they are progressing slowly but satisfactorily; nevertheless, if Jack would leave St. Petersburg, and come with me to London or New York, where he could carry on his experiments quite as well, or even better than here, I should depart at once, even if I jeopardized my own prospects."

The next letter, some time later, began:

"Your two charming notes to me arrived here together. It is very kind of you to write to a poor exile and cheer him in his banishment. I should like to see that dell where you have swung your hammock. Beware of Hendrick Hudson's men, so delightfully written of by Washington Irving. If they offer you anything to drink, don't you take it. Think how disastrous it would be to all your friends if you went to sleep in that hammock for twenty years. It's the Catskills I want to see now rather than Niagara Falls. Your second letter containing the note from Captain Kempt to Jack was at once delivered to him. What on earth has the genial Captain written to effect such a transformation in my friend? He came to me that evening clothed in his right mind; in evening rig-out, with his decorations upon it, commanded me to get into my dinner togs, took me in a carriage across the river to the best restaurant St. Petersburg affords, and there we had a champagne dinner in which he drank to America and all things American. Whether it was the enthusiasm produced

94

by Captain Kempt's communication, or the effect of the champagne, I do not know, but he has reconsidered his determination not to return to the United States, and very soon we set out together for the west.

"I shall be glad to get out of this place. We were followed to the restaurant, I am certain, and I am equally certain that at the next table two police spies were seated, and these two shadowed us in a cab until we reached our blacksmith's shop. It is a humiliating confession to make, but somehow the atmosphere of this place has got on my nerves, and I shall be glad to turn my back on it. Jack pooh-poohs the idea that he is in any danger. Even the Governor of St. Petersburg, he says, dare not lay a finger on him, and as for the Chief of Police, he pours scorn on that powerful official. He scouts the idea that he is being watched, and all-in-all is quite humorous at my expense, saying that my state of mind is more fitting for a schoolgirl than for a stalwart man over six feet in height. One consolation is that Jack now has become as keen for America as I am. I expect that the interview arranged for me to-morrow with a great government official will settle my own business finally one way or another. A while ago I was confident of success, but the repeated delays have made me less optimistic now, although the gentle courtesy of those in high places remains undiminished.

"Dear Miss Amhurst, I cannot afford to fall lower in your estimation than perhaps I deserve, so I must say that this fear which has overcome me is all on account of my friend, and not on my own behalf at all. I am perfectly safe in Russia, being a British subject. My cold and formal Cousin Thaxted is a member of the British Embassy here, and my cold and formal uncle is a Cabinet Minister in England, facts which must be well known to these spy-informed people of St. Petersburg; so I am immune. The worst they could do would be to order me out of the country, but even that is unthinkable. If any one attempted to interfere with me, I have only to act the hero of the penny novelette, draw myself up to my full height, which, as you know, is not that of a pigmy, fold my arms across my manly chest, cry, 'Ha, ha!' and sing 'Rule Britannia,' whereupon the villains would wilt and withdraw. But Jack has no such security. He is a Russian subject, and, prince or commoner, the authorities here could do what they liked with him. I always think of things when it is too late to act. I wish I had urged Jack ashore at Bar Harbor, and induced him to take the oath of allegiance to the United States. I spoke to him about that coming home in the carriage, and to my amazement he said he wished he had thought of it himself at the time we were over there.

"But enough of this. I daresay he is in no real danger after all. Nevertheless, I shall induce him to pack to-morrow, and we will make for London together, so my next letter will bear a British stamp, and I assure you the air of England will taste good to one benighted Britisher whose name is Alan Drummond."

# CHAPTER X —CALAMITY UNSEEN

THE habit of industry practised from childhood to maturity is not obliterated by an unexpected shower of gold. Dorothy was an early riser, and one morning, entering the parlor from her room she saw, lying upon the table, a letter with a Russian stamp, but addressed in an unknown hand to her friend Katherine Kempt. She surmised that here was the first communication from the Prince, and expected to learn all about it during the luncheon hour at the latest. But the morning and afternoon passed, and Katherine made no sign, which Dorothy thought was most unusual. All that day and the next Katherine went about silent, sedate and serious, never once quoting the humorous Mr. Gilbert. On the third morning Dorothy was surprised, emerging from her room, to see Katherine standing by the table, a black book in her hand. On the table lay a large package from New York, recently opened, displaying a number of volumes in what might be termed serious binding, leather or cloth, but none showing that high coloring which distinguishes the output of American fiction.

"Good-morning, Dorothy. The early bird is after the worm of science." She held forth the volume in her hand. "Steele's 'Fourteen-Weeks' Course in Chemistry,' an old book, but fascinatingly written. Dorothy," she continued with a sigh, "I want to talk seriously with you."

"About chemistry?" asked Dorothy.

"About men," said Katherine firmly, "and, incidentally, about women."

"An interesting subject, Kate, but you've got the wrong text-books. You should have had a parcel of novels instead."

Dorothy seated herself, and Katherine followed her example, Steele's "Fourteen-Weeks' Course" resting in her lap.

"Every man," began Katherine, "should have a guardian to protect him."

"From women?"

"From all things that are deceptive, and not what they seem."

"That sounds very sententious, Kate. What does it mean?"

"It means that man is a simpleton, easily taken in. He is too honest for crafty women, who delude him shamelessly."

"Whom have you been deluding, Kate?"

"Dorothy, I am a sneak."

Dorothy laughed.

"Indeed, Katherine, you are anything but that. You couldn't do a mean or ungenerous action if you tried your best."

"You think, Dorothy, I could reform?" she asked, breathlessly, leaning forward.

"Reform? You don't need to reform. You are perfectly delightful as you are, and I know no man who is worthy of you. That's a woman's opinion; one who knows you well, and there is nothing dishonest about the opinion, either, in spite of your tirade against our sex."

"Dorothy, three days ago, be the same more or less, I received a letter from John Lamont."

"Yes, I saw it on the table, and surmised it was from him."

"Did you? You were quite right. The reading of that letter has revolutionized my character. I am a changed woman, Dorothy, and thoroughly ashamed of myself. When I remember how I have deluded that poor, credulous young man, in making him believe I understood even the fringe of what he spoke about, it fills me with grief at my perfidy, but I am determined to amend my ways if hard study will do it, and when next I see him I shall talk to him worthily like a female Thomas A. Edison."

Again Dorothy laughed.

"Now, that's heartless of you, Dorothy. Don't you see I'm in deadly earnest? Must my former frivolity dog my steps through life? When I call to mind that I made fun to you of his serious purpose in life, the thought makes me cringe and despise myself."

"Nonsense, Kate, don't go to the other extreme. I remember nothing you have said that needs withdrawal. You have never made a malicious remark in your life, Kate. Don't make me defend you against yourself. You have determined, I take it, to plunge into the subjects which interest the man you are going to marry. That is a perfectly laudable ambition, and I am quite sure you will succeed."

"I know I don't deserve all that, Dorothy, but I like it just the same. I like people to believe in me, even if I sometimes lose faith in myself. May I read you an extract from his letter?"

"Don't if you'd rather not."

"I'd rather, Dorothy, if it doesn't weary you, but you will understand when you have heard it, in what a new light I regard myself."

The letter proved to be within the leaves of the late Mr. Steele's book on Chemistry, and from this volume she extracted it, pressed it for a moment against her breast with her open hand, gazing across at her friend.

"Dorothy, my first love-letter!"

She turned the crisp, thin pages, and began:

"'You may recollect that foot-note which you marked with red ink in the book you so kindly gave me on the subject of Catalysis, which did not pertain to the subject of the volume in question, and yet was so illuminative to any student of chemistry. They have done a great deal with Catalysis in Germany with amazing commercial results, but the subject is one so recent that I had not previously gone thoroughly into it.'"

Katherine paused in the reading, and looked across at her auditor, an expression almost of despair in her eloquent eyes.

"Dorothy, what under heaven is Catalysis?"

"Don't ask me," replied Dorothy, suppressing a laugh, struck by the ludicrousness of any young and beautiful woman pressing any such sentiments as these to her bosom.

"Have you ever heard of a Catalytic process, Dorothy?" beseeched Katherine. "It is one of the phrases he uses."

"Never; go on with the letter, Kate."

"'I saw at once that if I could use Catalytic process which would be instantaneous in its solidifying effect on my liquid limestone, instead of waiting upon slow evaporation, I could turn out building stone faster than one can make brick. You, I am sure, with your more alert mind, saw this when you marked that passage in red.'"

"Oh, Dorothy," almost whimpered Katherine, leaning back, "how can I go on? Don't you see what a sneak I am? It was bad enough to cozen with my heedless, random markings of the book, but to think that line of red ink might have been marked in his blood, for I nearly sent the poor boy to his death."

"Go on, Katherine, go on, go on!"

"'In my search for a Catalytic whose substance would remain unchanged after the reaction, I quite overlooked the chemical ingredients of one of the materials I was dealing with, and the result was an explosion which nearly blew the roof off the shop, and quite startled poor Drummond out of a year's growth. However, no real harm has been done, while I have been taught a valuable lesson; to take into account all the elements I am using. I must not become so intent on the subject I am pursuing as to ignore everything else.' And now, Dorothy, I want to ask you a most intimate question, which I beg of you to answer as frankly as I have confided in you."

"I know what your question is, Kate. A girl who is engaged wishes to see her friend in the same position. You would ask me if I am in love with Alan Drummond, and I answer perfectly frankly that I am not."

"You are quite sure of that, Dorothy?"

"Quite. He is the only man friend I have had, except my own father, and

I willingly confess to a sisterly interest in him."

"Well, if that is all—"

"It is all, Kate. Why?"

"Because there is something about him in this letter, which I would read to you if I thought you didn't care."

"Oh, he is in love with Jack's sister, very likely. I should think that would be a most appropriate arrangement. Jack is his best friend, and perhaps a lover would weaken the influence which Tolstoi exerts over an emotional person's mind. Lieutenant Drummond, with his sanity, would probably rescue a remnant of her estates."

"Oh, well, if you can talk as indifferently as that, you are all right, Dorothy. No, there is no other woman in the case. Here's what Jack says:

"'It is amazing how little an Englishman understands people of other nations. Here is my tall friend Drummond marching nonchalantly among dangers of which he has not the least conception. The authorities whom he thinks so courteous are fooling him to the top of his bent. There is, of course, no danger of his arrest, but nevertheless the eyes of the police are upon him, and he will not believe it, any more than he will believe he is being hoodwinked by the Foreign Minister. What I fear is that he will be bludgeoned on the street some dark night, or involved in a one-sided duel. Twice I have rescued him from an imminent danger which he has not even seen. Once in a restaurant a group of officers, apparently drunk, picked a quarrel and drew swords upon him. I had the less difficulty in getting him away because he fears a broil, or anything that will call down upon him the attention of his wooden-headed cousin in the Embassy. On another occasion as we were coming home toward midnight, a perfectly bogus brawl broke out suddenly all around us. Drummond was unarmed, but his huge fists sent sprawling two or three of his assailants. I had a revolver, and held the rest off, and so we escaped. I wish he was safely back in London again.' What do you think of that, Dorothy?"

"I think exactly what Mr. Lamont thinks. Lieutenant Drummond's mission to Russia seems to me a journey of folly."

"After all, I am glad you don't care, Dorothy. He should pay attention to what Jack says, for Jack knows Russia, and he doesn't. Still, let us hope he will come safely out of St. Petersburg. And now, Dot, for breakfast, because I must get to work."

Next morning Dorothy saw a letter for herself on the table in the now familiar hand-writing, and was more relieved than perhaps she would have confessed even to her closest friend, when she saw the twopence-halfpenny English stamp on the envelope. Yet its contents were startling enough, and this letter she did not read to Katherine Kempt, but bore its anxiety alone.

DEAR MISS AMHURST:

I write you in great trouble of mind, not trusting this letter to the Russian post-office, but sending it by an English captain to be posted in London. Two days ago Jack Lamont disappeared; a disappearance as complete as if he had never existed. The night before last, about ten o'clock, I thought I heard him come into his shop below my room. Sometimes he works there till daylight, and as, when absorbed in his experiments, he does not relish interruptions, even from me, I go on with my reading until he comes upstairs. Toward eleven o'clock I thought I heard slight sounds of a scuffle, and a smothered cry. I called out to him, but received no answer. Taking a candle, I went downstairs, but everything was exactly as usual, the doors locked, and not even a bench overturned. I called aloud, but only the echo of this barn of a room replied. I lit the gas and made a more intelligent search, but with no result. I unlocked the door, and stood out in the street, which was quite silent and deserted. I began to doubt that I had heard anything at all, for, as I have told you, my nerves lately have been rather prone to the jumps. I sat up all night waiting for him, but he did not come. Next day I went, as had been previously arranged, to the Foreign Office, but was kept waiting in an anteroom for two hours, and then told that the Minister could not see me. I met a similar repulse at the Admiralty. I dined alone at the restaurant Jack and I frequent, but saw nothing of him. This morning he has not returned, and I am at my wit's end, not in the least knowing what to do. It is useless

102

for me to appeal to the embassy of my country, for, Jack being a Russian, it has no jurisdiction. The last letter I received from you was tampered with. The newspaper extract you spoke of was not there, and one of the sheets of the letter was missing. Piffling business, I call it, this interfering with private correspondence.

Such was the last letter that Alan Drummond was ever to send to Dorothy Amhurst.

# CHAPTER XI — THE SNOW

SUMMER waned; the evenings became chill, although the sun pretended at noon that its power was undiminished. Back to town from mountain and sea shore filtered the warm-weather idlers, but no more letters came from St. Petersburg to the hill by the Hudson. So far as our girls were concerned, a curtain of silence had fallen between Europe and America.

The flat was now furnished, and the beginning of autumn saw it occupied by the two friends. Realization in this instance lacked the delight of anticipation. At last Katherine was the bachelor girl she had longed to be, but the pleasures of freedom were as Dead Sea fruit to the lips. At last Dorothy was effectually cut off from all thoughts of slavery, with unlimited money to do what she pleased with, yet after all, of what advantage was it in solving the problem that haunted her by day and filled her dreams by night. She faced the world with seeming unconcern, for she had not the right to mourn, even if she knew he were dead. He had made no claim; had asked for no affection; had written no word to her but what all the world might read. Once a week she made a little journey up the Hudson to see how her church was coming on, and at first Katherine accompanied her, but now she went alone. Katherine was too honest a girl to pretend an interest where she felt none. She could not talk of architecture when she was thinking of a man and his fate. At first she had been querulously impatient when no second communication came. Her own letters, she said, must have reached him, otherwise they would have been returned. Later, dumb fear took possession of her, and she grew silent, plunged with renewed energy into her books, joined a technical school, took lessons, and grew paler and paler until her teachers warned her she was overdoing it. Inwardly she resented the serene impassiveness of her friend, who consulted calmly with the architect upon occasion about the decoration of the church, when men's liberty was gone, and perhaps their lives. She built up within her mind a romance of devotion, by which her lover, warning in vain the stolid Englishman, had at last been involved in the ruin that Drummond's stubbornness had brought upon them both, and unjustly implicated the quiet woman by her side in the responsibility of this sacrifice. Once or twice she spoke with angry impatience of Drummond and his stupidity, but Dorothy neither defended nor excused, and so no open rupture occurred between the two friends, for a quarrel cannot be one-sided.

But with a woman of Katherine's temperament the final outburst had to come, and it came on the day that the first flurry of snow fell through the still air, capering in large flakes past the windows of the flat down to the muddy street far below. Katherine was standing by the window, with her forehead leaning against the plate glass, in exactly the attitude that had been her habit in the sewing-room at Bar Harbor, but now the staccato of her fingers on the sill seemed to drum a Dead March of despair. The falling snow had darkened the room, and one electric light was aglow over the dainty Chippendale desk at which Dorothy sat writing a letter. The smooth, regular flow of the pen over the paper roused Katherine to a frenzy of exasperation. Suddenly she brought her clenched fist down on the sill where her fingers had been drumming.

"My God," she cried, "how can you sit there like an automaton with the snow falling?"

Dorothy put down her pen.

"The snow falling?" she echoed. "I don't understand!"

"Of course you don't. You don't think of the drifts in Siberia, and the two men you have known, whose hands you have clasped, manacled, driven through it with the lash of a Cossack's whip."

Dorothy rose quietly, and put her hands on the shoulders of the girl, feeling her frame tremble underneath her touch.

"Katherine," she said, quietly, but Katherine, with a nervous twitch of her shoulders flung off the friendly grasp.

"Don't touch me," she cried. "Go back to your letter-writing. You and the Englishman are exactly alike; unfeeling, heartless. He with his selfish stubbornness has involved an innocent man in the calamity his own stupidity has brought about."

"Katherine, sit down. I want to talk calmly with you."

"Calmly! Calmly! Yes, that is the word. It is easy for you to be calm when you don't care. But I care, and I cannot be calm."

"What do you wish to do, Katherine?"

"What can I do? I am a pauper and a dependent, but one thing I am determined to do, and that is to go and live in my father's house."

"If you were in my place, what would you do Katherine?"

"I would go to Russia."

"What would you do when you arrived there?"

"If I had wealth I would use it in such a campaign of bribery and corruption in that country of tyrants that I should release two innocent men. I'd first find out where they were, then I'd use all the influence I possessed with the American Ambassador to get them set free."

"The American Ambassador, Kate, cannot move to release either an Englishman or a Russian."

"I'd do it somehow. I wouldn't sit here like a stick or a stone, writing letters to my architect."

"Would you go to Russia alone?"

"No, I should take my father with me."

"That is an excellent idea, Kate. I advise you to go north by to-night's train, if you like, and see him, or telegraph to him to come and see us."

Kate sat down, and Dorothy drew the curtains across the window pane and snapped on the central cluster of electric lamps.

"Will you come with me if I go north?" asked Kate, in a milder tone than she had hitherto used.

"I cannot. I am making an appointment with a man in this room to-morrow."

"The architect, I suppose," cried Kate with scorn.

"No, with a man who may or may not give me information of Lamont or Drummond."

Katherine stared at her open-eyed.

"Then you have been doing something?"

"I have been trying, but it is difficult to know what to do. I have received information that the house in which Mr. Lamont and Mr. Drummond lived is now deserted, and no one knows anything of its former occupants. That information comes to me semi-officially, but it does not lead far. I have started inquiry through more questionable channels; in other words, I have invoked the aid of a Nihilist society, and although I am quite determined to go to Russia with you, do not be surprised if I am arrested the moment I set foot in St. Petersburg."

"Dorothy, why did you not let me know?"

"I was anxious to get some good news to give you, but it has not come yet."

"Oh, Dorothy," moaned Katherine, struggling to keep back the tears that would flow in spite of her. Dorothy patted her on the shoulder.

"You have been a little unjust," she said, "and I am going to prove that to you, so that in trying to make amends you may perhaps stop brooding over this crisis that faces two poor lone women. You wrong the Englishman, as you call him. Jack was arrested at least two days before he was. Nihilist spies say that both of them were arrested, the Prince first, and the Englishman several days later. I had a letter from Mr. Drummond a short time after you received yours from Mr. Lamont. I never showed it to you, but now things are so bad that they cannot be worse, and you are at liberty to read the letter if you wish to do so. It tells of Jack's disappearance, and of Drummond's agony of mind and helplessness in St. Petersburg. Since he has never written again, I am sure he was arrested later. I don't know which of the two was most at fault for what you call stubbornness, but I believe the explosion had more to do with the arrests than any action of theirs."

"And I was the cause of that," wailed Katherine.

"No, no, my dear girl. No one is to blame but the tyrant of Russia. Now the Nihilists insist that neither of these men has been sent to Siberia. They think they are in the prison of 'St. Peter and St. Paul.' That information came to me to-day in the letter I was just now answering. So, Katherine, I think you have been unjust to the Englishman. If he had been arrested first, there might be some grounds for what you charge, but they evidently gave him a chance to escape. He had his warning in the disappearance of his friend, and he had several days in which to get out of St. Petersburg, but he stood his ground."

"I'm sorry, Dorothy. I'm a silly fool, and to-day, when I saw the snow—well, I got all wrought up."

"I think neither of the men are in the snow, and now I am going to say something else, and then never speak of the subject again. You say I didn't care, and of course you are quite right, for I confessed to you that I didn't. But just imagine—imagine—that I cared. The Russian Government can let the Prince go at any moment, and there's nothing more to be said. He has no redress, and must take the consequences of his nationality. But if the Russian Government have arrested the Englishman; if they have put him in the prison of 'St. Peter and St. Paul,' they dare not release him, unless they are willing to face war. The Russian Government can do nothing in his case but deny, demand proof, and obliterate all chance of the truth ever being known. Alan Drummond is doomed: they dare not release him. Now think for a moment how much worse my case would be than yours, if—if—" her voice quivered and broke for the moment, then with tightly clenched fists she recovered control of herself, and finished: "if I cared."

"Oh, Dorothy, Dorothy, Dorothy!" gasped Katherine, springing to her feet.

"No, no, don't jump at any false conclusion. We are both nervous wrecks this afternoon. Don't misunderstand me. I don't care—I don't care, except that I hate tyranny, and am sorry for the victims of it."

"Dorothy, Dorothy!"

"We need a sane man in the house, Kate. Telegraph for your father to come down and talk to us both. I must finish my letter to the Nihilist."

"Dorothy!" said Katherine, kissing her.

# CHAPTER XII —THE DREADED TROGZMONDOFF

THE Nihilist was shown into the dainty drawing room of the flat, and found Dorothy Amhurst alone, as he had stipulated, waiting for him. He was dressed in a sort of naval uniform and held a peaked cap in his hand, standing awkwardly there as one unused to luxurious surroundings. His face was bronzed with exposure to sun and storm, and although he appeared to be little more than thirty years of age his closely cropped hair was white. His eyes were light blue, and if ever the expression of a man's countenance betokened stalwart honesty, it was the face of this sailor. He was not in the least Dorothy's idea of a dangerous plotter.

"Sit down," she said, and he did so like a man ill at ease.

"I suppose Johnson is not your real name," she began.

"It is the name I bear in America, Madam."

"Do you mind my asking you some questions?"

"No, Madam, but if you ask me anything I am not allowed to answer I shall not reply."

"How long have you been in the United States?"

"Only a few months, Madam."

"How come you to speak English so well?"

"In my young days I shipped aboard a bark plying between Helsingfors and New York."

"You are a Russian?"

"I am a Finlander, Madam."

"Have you been a sailor all your life?"

"Yes, Madam. For a time I was an unimportant officer on board a battleship in the Russian Navy, until I was discovered to be a Nihilist, when I was cast into prison. I escaped last May, and came to New York."

"What have you been doing since you arrived here?"

"I was so fortunate as to become mate on the turbine yacht 'The Walrus,' owned by Mr. Stockwell."

"Oh, that's the multi-millionaire whose bank failed a month ago?"

"Yes, Madam."

"But does he still keep a yacht?"

"No, Madam. I think he has never been aboard this one, although it is probably the most expensive boat in these waters. I am told it cost anywhere from half a million to a million. She was built by Thornycroft, like a cruiser, with Parson's turbine engines in her. After the failure, Captain and crew were discharged, and I am on board as a sort of watchman until she is sold, but there is not a large market for a boat like 'The Walrus,' and I am told they will take the fittings out of her, and sell her as a cruiser to one of the South American republics."

"Well, Mr. Johnson, you ought to be a reliable man, if the Court has put you in charge of so valuable a property."

"I believe I am considered honest, Madam."

"Then why do you come to me asking ten thousand dollars for a letter which you say was written to me, and which naturally belongs to me?"

The man's face deepened into a mahogany brown, and he shifted his cap uneasily in his hands.

"Madam, I am not acting for myself. I am Secretary of the Russian Liberation Society. They, through their branch at St. Petersburg, have conducted some investigations on your behalf."

"Yes, for which I paid them very well."

Johnson bowed.

"Our object, Madam, is the repression of tyranny. For that we are in continual need of money. It is the poor, and not the millionaires, who subscribe to our fund. It has been discovered that you are a rich woman, who will never miss the money asked, and so the demand was made. Believe me, Madam, I am acting by the command of my comrades. I tried to persuade them to leave compensation to your own generosity, but they refused. If you consider their demand unreasonable, you have but to say so, and I will return and tell them your decision."

"Have you brought the letter with you?"

"Yes, Madam."

"Must I agree to your terms before seeing it?"

"Yes, Madam."

"Have you read it?"

"Yes, Madam."

"Do you think it worth ten thousand dollars?"

The sailor looked up at the decorated ceiling for several moments before he replied.

"That is a question I cannot answer," he said at last. "It all depends on what you think of the writer."

"Answer one more question. By whom is the letter signed?"

"There is no signature, Madam. It was found in the house where the two young men lived. Our people searched the house from top to bottom surreptitiously, and they think the writer was arrested before he had finished the letter. There is no address, and nothing to show for whom it is intended, except the phrase beginning, 'My dearest Dorothy.'"

The girl leaned back in her chair, and drew a long breath. "It is not for me," she said, hastily; then bending forward, she cried suddenly:

"I agree to your terms: give it to me."

112

The man hesitated, fumbling in his inside pocket.

"I was to get your promise in writing," he demurred.

"Give it to me, give it to me," she demanded. "I do not break my word."

He handed her the letter.

"My dearest Dorothy," she read, in writing well known to her. "You may judge my exalted state of mind when you see that I dare venture on such a beginning. I have been worrying myself and other people all to no purpose. I have received a letter from Jack this morning, and so suspicious had I grown that for a few moments I suspected the writing was but an imitation of his. He is a very impulsive fellow, and can think of only one thing at a time, which accounts for his success in the line of invention. He was telegraphed to that his sister was ill, and left at once to see her. I had allowed my mind to become so twisted by my fears for his safety that, as I tell you, I suspected the letter to be counterfeit at first. I telegraphed to his estate, and received a prompt reply saying that his sister was much better, and that he was already on his way back, and would reach me at eleven to-night. So that's what happens when a grown man gets a fit of nerves. I drew the most gloomy conclusions from the fact that I had been refused admission to the Foreign Office and the Admiralty. Yesterday that was all explained away. The business is at last concluded, and I was shown copies of the letters which have been forwarded to my own chiefs at home. Nothing could be more satisfactory. To-morrow Jack and I will be off to England together.

"My dearest Dorothy (second time of asking), I am not a rich man, but then, in spite of your little fortune of Bar Harbor, you are not a rich woman, so we stand on an equality in that, even though you are so much my superior in everything else. I have five hundred pounds a year, which is something less than two thousand five hundred dollars, left me by my father. This is independent of my profession. I am very certain I will succeed in the Navy now that the Russian Government has sent those letters, so, the moment I was assured of that, I determined to write and ask you to be my wife. Will you forgive my impatience, and pander to it by cabling to me at the Bluewater Club, Pall Mall, the word 'Yes' or the word 'Undecided'? I shall not allow you the privilege of cabling 'No.' And please give me a chance of pleading my case in person, if you use the longer word. Ah, I hear Jack's step on the stair. Very stealthily he is coming, to surprise me, but I'll surprise—"

Here the writing ended. She folded the letter, and placed it in her desk, sitting down before it.

"Shall I make the check payable to you, or to the Society?"

"To the Society, if you please, Madam."

"I shall write it for double the amount asked. I also am a believer in liberty."

"Oh, Madam, that is a generosity I feel we do not deserve. I should like to have given you the letter after all you have done for us with no conditions attached."

"I am quite sure of that," said Dorothy, bending over her writing. She handed him the check, and he rose to go.

"Sit down again, if you please. I wish to talk further with you. Your people in St. Petersburg think my friends have not been sent to Siberia? Are they sure of that?"

"Well, Madam, they have means of knowing those who are transported, and they are certain the two young men were not among the recent gangs sent. They suppose them to be in the fortress of 'St. Peter and St. Paul', at least that's what they say."

"You speak as if you doubted it."

"I do doubt it."

"They have been sent to Siberia after all?"

"Ah, Madam, there are worse places than Siberia. In Siberia there is a chance: in the dreadful Trogzmondoff there is none."

"What is the Trogzmondoff?"

"A bleak 'Rock in the Baltic,' Madam, the prison in which death is the

114

only goal that releases the victim."

Dorothy rose trembling, staring at him, her lips white.

"'A Rock in the Baltic!' Is that a prison, and not a fortress, then?"

"It is both prison and fortress, Madam. If Russia ever takes the risk of arresting a foreigner, it is to the Trogzmondoff he is sent. They drown the victims there; drown them in their cells. There is a spring in the rock, and through the line of cells it runs like a beautiful rivulet, but the pulling of a lever outside stops the exit of the water, and drowns every prisoner within. The bodies are placed one by one on a smooth, inclined shute of polished sandstone, down which this rivulet runs so they glide out into space, and drop two hundred feet into the Baltic Sea. No matter in what condition such a body is found, or how recent may have been the execution, it is but a drowned man in the Baltic. There are no marks of bullet or strangulation, and the currents bear them swiftly away from the rock."

"How come you to know all this which seems to have been concealed from the rest of the world?"

"I know it, Madam, for the best of reasons. I was sentenced this very year to Trogzmondoff. In my youth trading between Helsingfors and New York, I took out naturalization papers in New York, because I was one of the crew on an American ship. When they illegally impressed me at Helsingfors and forced me to join the Russian Navy, I made the best of a bad bargain, and being an expert seaman, was reasonably well treated, and promoted, but at last they discovered I was in correspondence with a Nihilist circle in London, and when I was arrested, I demanded the rights of an American citizen. That doomed me. I was sent, without trial, to the Trogzmondoff in April of this year. Arriving there I was foolish enough to threaten, and say my comrades had means of letting the United States Government know, and that a battleship would teach the gaolers of the rock better manners.

"The cells hewn in the rock are completely dark, so I lost all count of time. You might think we would know night from day by the bringing in of our meals, but such was not the case. The gaoler brought in a large loaf of black bread, and said it was to serve me for four days. He placed the loaf on a ledge of rock about three feet from the floor, which served as both table and bed. In excavating the cell this ledge had been left intact, with a bench of stone rising from the floor opposite. Indeed, so ingenious had been the workmen who hewed out this room that they carved a rounded stone pillow at one end of the shelf.

"I do not know how many days I had been in prison when the explosion occurred. It made the whole rock quiver, and I wondered what had happened. Almost immediately afterward there seemed to be another explosion, not nearly so harsh, which I thought was perhaps an echo of the first. About an hour later my cell door was unlocked, and the gaoler, with another man holding a lantern, came in. My third loaf of black bread was partly consumed, so I must have been in prison nine or ten days. The gaoler took the loaf outside, and when he returned. I asked him what had happened. He answered in a surly fashion that my American warship had fired at the rock, and that the rock had struck back, whereupon she sailed away, crippled."

Dorothy, who had been listening intently to this discourse, here interrupted with:

"It was an English war-ship that fired the shell, and the Russian shot did not come within half a mile of her."

The sailor stared at her in wide-eyed surprise.

"You see, I have been making inquiries," she explained. "Please go on."

"I never heard that it was an English ship. The gaoler sneered at me, and said he was going to send me after the American vessel, as I suppose he thought it was. I feared by his taking away of the bread that it was intended to starve me to death, and was sorry I had not eaten more at my last meal. I lay down on the shelf of rock, and soon fell asleep. I was awakened by the water lapping around me. The cell was intensely still. Up to this I had always enjoyed the company of a little brook that ran along the side of the cell farthest from the door. Its music had now ceased, and when I sprang up I found myself to the waist in very cold water. I guessed at once the use of the levers outside the cell in the passage which I had noticed in the light of the lantern on the day I entered the place, and I knew now why it was that the prison door was not pierced by one of those gratings which enable the gaoler in the passage to look into the cell any time of night or day. Prisoners have told me that the uncertainty of an inmate who never knew when he might be spied upon added to the horror of the situation, but the water-tight doors of the Trogzmondoff are free from this feature, and for a very sinister reason.

"The channel in the floor through which the water runs when the cell is empty, and the tunnel at the ceiling through which the water flows when the cell is full, give plenty of ventilation, no matter how tightly the door may be closed. The water rose very gradually until it reached the top outlet, then its level remained stationary. I floated on the top quite easily, with as little exertion as was necessary to keep me in that position. If I raised my head, my brow struck the ceiling. The next cell to mine, lower down, was possibly empty. I heard the water pour into it like a little cataract. The next cell above, and indeed all the cells in that direction were flooded like my own. Of course it was no trouble for me to keep afloat; my only danger was that the intense coldness of the water would numb my body beyond recovery. Still, I had been accustomed to hardships of that kind before now, in the frozen North. At last the gentle roar of the waterfall ceased, and I realized my cell was emptying itself. When I reached my shelf again, I stretched my limbs back and forth as strenuously as I could, and as silently, for I wished no sound to give any hint that I was still alive, if, indeed, sound could penetrate to the passage, which is unlikely. Even before the last of the water had run away from the cell, I lay stretched out at full length on the floor, hoping I might have steadiness enough to remain death-quiet when the men came in with the lantern. I need have had no fear. The door was opened, one of the men picked me up by the heels, and, using my legs as if they were the shafts of a wheelbarrow, dragged me down the passage to the place where the stream emerged from the last cell, and into this torrent he flung me. There was one swift, brief moment of darkness, then I shot, feet first, into space, and dropped down, down, down through the air like a plummet, into the arms of my mother."

"Into what?" cried Dorothy, white and breathless, thinking the recital of these agonies had turned the man's brain.

"The Baltic, Madam, is the Finlander's mother. It feeds him in life, carries him whither he wishes to go, and every true Finlander hopes to die in her arms. The Baltic seemed almost warm after what I had been through, and the taste of the salt on my lips was good. It was a beautiful starlight night in May, and I floated around the rock, for I knew that in a cove on the eastern side, concealed from all view of the sea, lay a Finland fishing-boat, a craft that will weather any storm, and here in the water was a man who knew how to handle it. Prisoners are landed on the eastern side, and such advantage is taken of the natural conformation of this precipitous rock, that a man climbing the steep zigzag stairway which leads to the inhabited portion is hidden from sight of any craft upon the water even four or five hundred yards away. Nothing seen from the outside gives any token of habitation. The fishing-boat, I suppose, is kept for cases of emergency, that the Governor may communicate with the shore if necessary. I feared it might be moored so securely that I could not unfasten it. Security had made them careless, and the boat was tied merely by lines to rings in the rock, the object being to keep her from bruising her sides against the stone, rather than to prevent any one taking her away. I pushed her out into the open, got quietly inside, and floated with the swift tide, not caring to raise a sail until I was well out of gunshot distance. Once clear of the rock I spread canvas, and by daybreak was long out of sight of land. I made for Stockholm, and there being no mark or name on the boat to denote that it belonged to the Russian Government, I had little difficulty in selling it. I told the authorities what was perfectly true: that I was a Finland sailor escaping from the tyrant of my country, and anxious to get to America. As such events are happening practically every week along the Swedish coast I was not interfered with, and got enough money from the sale of the boat to enable me to dress myself well, and take passage to England, and from there first-class to New York on a regular liner.

"Of course I could have shipped as a sailor from Stockholm easy enough, but I was tired of being a common sailor, and expected, if I was respectably clothed, to get a better position than would otherwise be the case. This proved true, for crossing the ocean I became acquainted with Mr. Stockwell, and he engaged me as mate of his yacht. That's how I escaped from the Trogzmondoff, Madam, and I think no one but a Finlander could have done it."

"I quite agree with you," said Dorothy. "You think these two men I have been making inquiry about have been sent to the Trogzmondoff?"

"The Russian may not be there, Madam, but the Englishman is sure to be there."

"Is the cannon on the western side of the rock?"

"I don't know, Madam. I never saw the western side by daylight. I noticed nothing on the eastern side as I was climbing the steps, to show that any cannon was on the Trogzmondoff at all."

"I suppose you had no opportunity of finding out how many men garrison the rock?"

"No, Madam. I don't think the garrison is large. The place is so secure that it doesn't need many men to guard it. Prisoners are never taken out for exercise, and, as I told you, they are fed but once in four days."

"How large a crew can 'The Walrus' carry?"

"Oh, as many as you like, Madam. The yacht is practically an ocean liner."

"Is there any landing stage on the eastern side of the rock?"

"Practically none, Madam. The steamer stood out, and I was landed in the cove I spoke of at the foot of the stairway."

"It wouldn't be possible to bring a steamer like 'The Walrus' alongside the rock, then?"

"It would be possible in calm weather, but very dangerous even then."

"Could you find that rock if you were in command of a ship sailing the Baltic?"

"Oh, yes, Madam."

"If twenty or thirty determined men were landed on the stairway, do you think they could capture the garrison?"

"Yes, if they were landed secretly, but one or two soldiers at the top with repeating rifles might hold the stairway against an army, while their ammunition lasted."

"But if a shell were fired from the steamer, might not the attacking company get inside during the confusion among the defenders?"

"That is possible, Madam, but a private steamer firing shells, or, indeed, landing a hostile company, runs danger of meeting the fate of a pirate."

"You would not care to try it, then?"

"I? Oh, I should be delighted to try it, if you allow me to select the crew. I can easily get aboard the small arms and ammunition necessary, but I am not so sure about the cannon."

"Very good. I need not warn you to be extremely cautious regarding those you take into your confidence. Meanwhile, I wish you to communicate with the official who is authorized to sell the yacht. I am expecting a gentleman to-morrow in whose name the vessel will probably be bought, and I am hoping he will accept the captaincy of it."

"Is he capable of filling that position, Madam? Is he a sailor?"

"He was for many years captain in the United States Navy. I offer you the position of mate, but I will give you captain's pay, and a large bonus in addition if you faithfully carry out my plans, whether they prove successful or not. I wish you to come here at this hour to-morrow, with whoever is authorized to sell or charter the steamer. You may say I am undecided whether to buy or charter. I must consult Captain Kempt on that point."

"Thank you, Madam, I shall be here this time to-morrow."

# CHAPTER XIII —ENTRAPPED

PRINCE IVAN LERMONTOFF came to consider the explosion one of the luckiest things that had ever occurred in his workshop. Its happening so soon after he reached St. Petersburg he looked upon as particularly fortunate, because this gave him time to follow the new trend of thought along which his mind had been deflected by such knowledge as the unexpected outcome of his experiment had disclosed to him. The material he had used as a catalytic agent was a new substance which he had read of in a scientific review, and he had purchased a small quantity of it in London. If such a minute portion produced results so tremendous, he began to see that a man with an apparently innocent material in his waistcoat pocket might probably be able to destroy a naval harbor, so long as water and stone were in conjunction. There was also a possibility that a small quantity of ozak, as the stuff was called, mixed with pure water, would form a reducing agent for limestone, and perhaps for other minerals, which would work much quicker than if the liquid was merely impregnated with carbonic acid gas. He endeavored to purchase some ozak from Mr. Kruger, the chemist on the English quay, but that good man had never heard of it, and a day's search persuaded him that it could not be got in St. Petersburg, so the Prince induced Kruger to order half a pound of it from London or Paris, in which latter city it had been discovered. For the arrival of this order the Prince waited with such patience as he could call to his command, and visited poor Mr. Kruger every day in the hope of receiving it.

One afternoon he was delighted to hear that the box had come, although it had not yet been unpacked.

"I will send it to your house this evening," said the chemist. "There are a number of drugs in the box for your old friend Professor Potkin of the University, and he is even more impatient for his consignment than you are for yours. Ah, here he is," and as he spoke the venerable Potkin himself entered the shop.

He shook hands warmly with Lermontoff, who had always been a favorite pupil of his, and learned with interest that he had lately been to England and America.

"Cannot you dine with me this evening at half-past five?" asked the old man. "There are three or four friends coming, to whom I shall be glad to introduce you."

"Truth to tell, Professor," demurred the Prince, "I have a friend staying with me, and I don't just like to leave him alone."

"Bring him with you, bring him with you," said the Professor, "but in any case be sure you come yourself. I shall be expecting you. Make your excuses to your friend if he does not wish to endure what he might think dry discussion, because we shall talk nothing but chemistry and politics."

The Prince promised to be there whether his friend came or no. The chemist here interrupted them, and told the Professor he might expect his materials within two hours.

"And your package," he said to the Prince, "I shall send about the same time. I have been very busy, and can trust no one to unpack this box but myself."

"You need not trouble to send it, and in any case I don't wish to run the risk of having it delivered at a wrong address by your messenger. I cannot afford to wait so long as would be necessary to duplicate the order. I am dining with the Professor to-night, so will drive this way, and take the parcel myself."

"Perhaps," said the chemist, "it would be more convenient if I sent your parcel to Professor Potkin's house?"

"No," said the Prince decisively, "I shall call for it about five o'clock."

The Professor laughed.

"We experimenters," he said, "never trust each other," so they shook hands and parted.

On returning to his workshop, Lermontoff bounded up the stairs, and hailed his friend the Lieutenant.

"I say, Drummond, I'm going to dine to-night with Professor Potkin of the University, my old teacher in chemistry. His hour is half-past five, and I've got an invitation for you. There will be several scientists present, and no women. Will you come?"

"I'd a good deal rather not," said the Englishman, "I'm wiring into these books, and studying strategy; making plans for an attack upon Kronstadt."

"Well, you take my advice, Alan, and don't leave any of those plans round where the St. Petersburg police will find them. Such a line of study is carried on much safer in London than here. You'd be very welcome, Drummond, and the old boy would be glad to see you. You don't need to bother about evening togs—plain living and high thinking, you know. I'm merely going to put on a clean collar and a new tie, as sufficient for the occasion."

"I'd rather not go, Jack, if you don't mind. If I'm there you'll all be trying to talk English or French, and so I'd feel myself rather a damper on the company. Besides, I don't know anything about science, and I'm trying to learn something about strategy. What time do you expect to be back?"

"Rather early; ten or half-past."

"Good, I'll wait up for you."

At five o'clock Jack was at the chemist's and received his package. On opening it he found the ozak in two four-ounce, glass-stoppered bottles, and these he put in his pocket.

"Will you give me three spray syringes, as large a size as you have, rubber, glass, and metal. I'm not sure but this stuff will attack one or other of them, and I don't want to spend the rest of my life running down to your shop."

Getting the syringes, he jumped into his cab, and was driven to the Professor's.

"You may call for me at ten," he said to the cabman.

There were three others besides the Professor and himself, and they were all interested in learning the latest scientific news from New York and London.

It was a quarter past ten when the company separated. Lermontoff stepped into his cab, and the driver went rattling up the street. In all the talk the Prince had said nothing of his own discovery, and now when he found himself alone his mind reverted to the material in his pocket, and he was glad the cabman was galloping his horse, that he might be the sooner in his workshop. Suddenly he noticed that they were dashing down a street which ended at the river.

"I say," he cried to the driver, "you've taken the wrong turning. This is a blind street. There's neither quay nor bridge down here. Turn back."

"I see that now," said the driver over his shoulder. "I'll turn round at the end where it is wider."

He did turn, but instead of coming up the street again, dashed through an open archway which led into the courtyard of a large building fronting the Neva. The moment the carriage was inside, the gates clanged shut.

"Now, what in the name of Saint Peter do you mean by this?" demanded the Prince angrily.

The cabman made no reply, but from a door to the right stepped a tall, uniformed officer, who said:

"Orders, your Highness, orders. The isvoshtchik is not to blame. May I beg of your Highness to accompany me inside?"

"Who the devil are you?" demanded the annoyed nobleman.

"I am one who is called upon to perform a disagreeable duty, which your Highness will make much easier by paying attention to my requests."

"Am I under arrest?"

"I have not said so, Prince Ivan."

"Then I demand that the gates be opened that I may return home, where more important business awaits me than talking to a stranger who refuses to reveal his identity."

"I hope you will pardon me, Prince Lermontoff. I act, as the isvoshtchik has acted, under compulsion. My identity is not in question. I ask you for the second time to accompany me."

"Then, for the second time I inquire, am I under arrest? If so, show me your warrant, and then I will go with you, merely protesting that whoever issued such a warrant has exceeded his authority."

"I have seen nothing of a warrant, your Highness, and I think you are confusing your rights with those pertaining to individuals residing in certain countries you have recently visited."

"You have no warrant, then?"

"I have none. I act on my superior's word, and do not presume to question it. May I hope that you will follow me without a further parley, which is embarrassing to me, and quite unhelpful to yourself. I have been instructed to treat you with every courtesy, but nevertheless force has been placed at my disposal. I am even to take your word of honor that you are unarmed, and your Highness is well aware that such leniency is seldom shown in St. Petersburg."

"Well, sir, even if my word of honor failed to disarm me, your politeness would. I carry a revolver. Do you wish it?"

"If your Highness will condescend to give it to me."

The Prince held the weapon, butt forward, to the officer, who received it with a gracious salutation.

"You know nothing of the reason for this action?"

"Nothing whatever, your Highness."

"Where are you going to take me?"

"A walk of less than three minutes will acquaint your Highness with the

125

spot."

The Prince laughed.

"Oh, very well," he said. "May I write a note to a friend who is waiting up for me?"

"I regret, Highness, that no communications whatever can be allowed."

The Prince stepped down from the vehicle, walked diagonally across a very dimly lighted courtyard with his guide, entered that section of the rectangular building which faced the Neva, passed along a hall with one gas jet burning, then outside again, and immediately over a gang-plank that brought him aboard a steamer. On the lower deck a passage ran down the center of the ship, and along this the conductor guided his prisoner, opened the door of a stateroom in which candles were burning, and a comfortable bed turned down for occupancy.

"I think your Highness will find everything here that you need. If anything further is required, the electric bell will summon an attendant, who will get it for you."

"Am I not to be confronted with whoever is responsible for my arrest?"

"I know nothing of that, your Highness. My duty ends by escorting you here. I must ask if you have any other weapon upon you?"

"No, I have not."

"Will you give me your parole that you will not attempt to escape?"

"I shall escape if I can, of course."

"Thank you, Excellency," replied the officer, as suavely as if Lermontoff had given his parole. Out of the darkness he called a tall, rough-looking soldier, who carried a musket with a bayonet at the end of it. The soldier took his stand beside the door of the cabin.

"Anything else?" asked the Prince.

"Nothing else, your Highness, except good-night."

"Oh, by the way, I forgot to pay my cabman. Of course it isn't his fault that he brought me here."

"I shall have pleasure in sending him to you, and again, good-night."

"Good-night," said the Prince.

He closed the door of his cabin, pulled out his note-book, and rapidly wrote two letters, one of which he addressed to Drummond and the other to the Czar. When the cabman came he took him within the cabin and closed the door.

"Here," he said in a loud voice that the sentry could overhear if he liked, "how much do I owe you?"

The driver told him.

"That's too much, you scoundrel," he cried aloud, but as he did so he placed three gold pieces in the palm of the driver's hand together with the two letters, and whispered:

"Get these delivered safely, and I'll give you ten times this money if you call on Prince Lermontoff at the address on that note."

The man saluted, thanked him, and retired; a moment later he heard the jingle of a bell, and then the steady throb of an engine. There was no window to the stateroom, and he could not tell whether the steamer was going up or down the river. Up, he surmised, and he suspected his destination was Schlusselburg, the fortress-prison on an island at the source of the Neva. He determined to go on deck and solve the question of direction, but the soldier at the door brought down his gun and barred the passage.

"I am surely allowed to go on deck?"

"You cannot pass without an order from the captain."

"Well, send the captain to me, then."

"I dare not leave the door," said the soldier.

Lermontoff pressed the button, and presently an attendant came to learn what was wanted.

"Will you ask the captain to come here?"

The steward departed, and shortly after returned with a big, bronzed, bearded man, whose bulk made the stateroom seem small.

"You sent for the captain, and I am here."

"So am I," said the Prince jauntily. "My name is Lermontoff. Perhaps you have heard of me?"

The captain shook his shaggy head.

"I am a Prince of Russia, and by some mistake find myself your passenger instead of spending the night in my own house. Where are you taking me, Captain?"

"It is forbidden that I should answer questions."

"Is it also forbidden that I should go on deck?"

"The General said you were not to be allowed to leave this stateroom, as you did not give your parole."

"How can I escape from a steamer in motion, Captain?"

"It is easy to jump into the river, and perhaps swim ashore."

"So he is a general, is he? Well, Captain, I'll give you my parole that I shall not attempt to swim the Neva on so cold a night as this."

"I cannot allow you on deck now," said the Captain, "but when we are in the Gulf of Finland you may walk the deck with the sentry beside you."

"The Gulf of Finland!" cried Lermontoff. "Then you are going down the river?"

The big Captain looked at him with deep displeasure clouding his brow, feeling that he had been led to give away information which he should have kept to himself.

"You are not going up to Schlusselburg, then?"

"I told your Highness that I am not allowed to answer questions. The General, however, has given me a letter for you, and perhaps it may contain all you may want to know."

"The General has given you a letter, eh? Then why don't you let me have it?"

"He told me not to disturb you to-night, but place it before you at breakfast to-morrow."

"Oh, we're going to travel all night, are we?"

"Yes, Excellency."

"Did the General say you should not allow me to see the letter to-night?"

"No, your Excellency; he just said, 'Do not trouble his Highness to-night, but give him this in the morning.'"

"In that case let me have it now."

The Captain pulled a letter from his pocket and presented it to the Prince. It contained merely the two notes which Lermontoff had written to Drummond and to the Czar.

## CHAPTER XIV —A VOYAGE INTO THE UNKNOWN

AFTER the Captain left him, Lermontoff closed and bolted the door, then sat down upon the edge of his bed to meditate upon the situation. He heard distant bells ringing on shore somewhere, and looking at his watch saw it was just eleven o'clock. It seemed incredible that three-quarters of an hour previously he had left the hospitable doors of a friend, and now was churning his way in an unknown steamer to an unknown destination. It appeared impossible that so much could have happened in forty-five minutes. He wondered what Drummond was doing, and what action he would take when he found his friend missing.

However, pondering over the matter brought no solution of the mystery, so, being a practical young man, he cast the subject from his mind, picked up his heavy overcoat, which he had flung on the bed, and hung it up on the hook attached to the door. As he did this his hand came in contact with a tube in one of the pockets, and for a moment he imagined it was his revolver, but he found it was the metal syringe he had purchased that evening from the chemist. This set his thoughts whirling in another direction. He took from an inside pocket one of the bottles of ozak, examining it under the candle light, wishing he had a piece of rock with which to experiment. Then with a yawn he replaced the materials in his overcoat pocket, took off his boots, and threw himself on the bed, thankful it was not an ordinary shelf bunk, but a generous and comfortable resting-place. Now Katherine appeared before his closed eyes, and hand in hand they wandered into dreamland together.

When he awoke it was pitch dark in his cabin. The candles, which he had neglected to extinguish, had burned themselves out. The short, jerky motion of the steamer indicated that he was aboard a small vessel, and that this small vessel was out in the open sea. He believed that a noise of some kind had awakened him, and this was confirmed by a knock at his door which caused him to spring up and throw back the bolt. The steward was there, but in the dim light of the passage he saw nothing of the sentinel. He knew it was daylight outside.

"The Captain, Excellency, wishes to know if you will breakfast with him or take your meal in your room?"

"Present my compliments to the Captain, and say I shall have great pleasure in breakfasting with him."

"It will be ready in a quarter of an hour, Excellency."

"Very good. Come for me at that time, as I don't know my way about the boat."

The Prince washed himself, smoothed out his rumpled clothes as well as he could, and put on his boots. While engaged in the latter operation the door opened, and the big Captain himself entered, inclosed in glistening oilskins.

"Hyvaa pyvaa, Highness," said the Captain. "Will you walk the deck before breakfast?"

"Good-day to you," returned the Prince, "and by your salutation I take you to be a Finn."

"I am a native of Abo," replied the Captain, "and as you say, a Finn, but I differ from many of my countrymen, as I am a good Russian also."

"Well, there are not too many good Russians, and here is one who would rather have heard that you were a good Finn solely."

"It is to prevent any mistake," replied the Captain, almost roughly, "that I mention I am a good Russian."

"Right you are, Captain, and as I am a good Russian also, perhaps good Russian Number One can tell me to what part of the world he is conveying good Russian Number Two, a man guiltless of any crime, and unwilling, at this moment, to take an enforced journey."

"We may both be good, but the day is not, Highness. It has been raining during the night, and is still drizzling. I advise you to put on your overcoat."

"Thanks, Captain, I will."

The Captain in most friendly manner took the overcoat from its hook, shook it out, and held it ready to embrace its owner. Lermontoff shoved right arm, then left, into the sleeves, hunched the coat up into place, and buttoned it at the throat.

"Again, Captain, my thanks. Lead the way and I will follow."

They emerged on deck into a dismal gray morning. No land or craft of any kind was in sight. The horizon formed a small, close circle round the ship. Clouds hung low, running before the wind, and bringing intermittently little dashes of rain that seemed still further to compress the walls of horizon. The sea was not what could be called rough, but merely choppy and fretful, with short waves that would not have troubled a larger craft. The steamer proved to be a small, undistinguished dingy-looking boat, more like a commercial tramp than a government vessel. An officer, apparently the mate, stood on the bridge, sinewy hands grasping the rail, peering ahead into the white mist that was almost a fog. The promenade deck afforded no great scope for pedestrianism, but Captain and prisoner walked back and forth over the restricted space, talking genially together as if they were old friends. Nevertheless there was a certain cautious guardedness in the Captain's speech; the wary craft of an unready man who is in the presence of a person more subtle than himself. The bluff Captain remembered he had been caught napping the night before, when, after refusing to tell the Prince the direction of the steamer, he had given himself away by mentioning the Gulf of Finland. Lermontoff noticed this reluctance to plunge into the abyss of free conversation, and so, instead of reassuring him he would ask no more questions, he merely took upon his own shoulders the burden of the talk, and related to the Captain certain wonders of London and New York.

The steward advanced respectfully to the Captain, and announced breakfast ready, whereupon the two men followed him into a saloon not much larger than the stateroom Lermontoff had occupied the night before, and not nearly so comfortably furnished. A plenteous breakfast was supplied, consisting principally of fish, steaming potatoes, black bread, and very strong

132

tea. The Captain swallowed cup after cup of this scalding beverage, and it seemed to make him more and more genial as if it had been wine. Indeed, as time went on he forgot that it was a prisoner who sat before him, for quite innocently he said to the steward who waited on them:

"Have the poor devils below had anything to eat?"

"No orders, sir," replied the steward.

"Oh, well, give them something—something hot. It may be their last meal," then turning, he met the gaze of the Prince, demanded roughly another cup of tea, and explained:

"Three of the crew took too much vodka in St. Petersburg yesterday."

The Prince nodded carelessly, as if he believed, and offered his open cigarette case to the Captain, who shook his head.

"I smoke a pipe," he growled.

The Captain rose with his lighted pipe, and together they went up on deck again. The Prince saw nothing more of the tall sentinel who had been his guard the night before, so without asking permission he took it for granted that his movements, now they were in the open sea, were unrestricted, therefore he walked up and down the deck smoking cigarettes. At the stroke of a bell the Captain mounted the bridge and the mate came down.

Suddenly out of the thickness ahead loomed up a great black British freighter making for St. Petersburg, as the Prince supposed. The two steamers, big and little, were so close that each was compelled to sheer off a bit; then the Captain turned on the bridge and seemed for a moment uncertain what to do with his prisoner. A number of men were leaning over the bulwarks of the British ship, and it would have been quite possible for the person on one boat to give a message to those on the other. The Prince, understanding the Captain's quandary, looked up at him and smiled, but made no attempt to take advantage of his predicament. Some one on board the English ship shouted and fluttered a handkerchief, whereupon the Prince waved his cigarette in the air, and the big boat disappeared in the thickness of the east.

Lermontoff walked the deck, thinking very seriously about his situation, and wondering where they intended to take him. If he were to be put in prison, it must be in some place of detention on the coast of Finland, which seemed strange, because he understood that the fortresses there were already filled with dissatisfied inhabitants of that disaffected land. His first impression had been that banishment was intended, and he had expected to be landed at some Swedish or German port, but a chance remark made by the Captain at breakfast inclined him to believe that there were other prisoners on board not quite so favorably treated as himself. But why should he be sent out of Russia proper, or even removed from St. Petersburg, which, he was well aware, suffered from no lack of gaols. The continued voyage of the steamer through an open sea again aroused the hope that Stockholm was the objective point. If they landed him there it merely meant a little temporary inconvenience, and, once ashore, he hoped to concoct a telegram so apparently innocent that it would win through to his friend, and give Drummond at least the knowledge of his abiding-place. The thought of Drummond aroused all his old fear that the Englishman was to be the real victim, and this enforced voyage was merely a convenient method of getting himself out of the way.

After lunch a dismal drizzle set in that presently increased to a steady downpour, which drove Lermontoff to his cabin, and that room being unprovided with either window or electric light, the Prince struck a match to one of the candles newly placed on the washstand. He pushed the electric button summoning the steward, and, giving him some money, asked if there was such a thing as a piece of stone on board, carried as ballast, or for any other reason. The steward said he would inquire, and finally returned with a sharpening stone used for the knives in the galley. Bolting his door, Lermontoff began an experiment, and at once forgot he was a prisoner. He filled the wash-basin with water, and opening one of the glass-stoppered bottles, took out with the point of his knife a most minute portion of the substance within, which he dissolved in the water with no apparent effect. Standing the whetstone up on end, he filled the glass syringe, and directed a fine, vaporous spray against the stone. It dissolved before his eyes as a sand castle on the shore dissolves at the touch of an incoming tide.

"By St. Peter of Russia!" he cried, "I've got it at last! I must write to

Katherine about this."

Summoning the steward again to take away this fluid, and bring him another pailful of fresh water, Lermontoff endeavored to extract some information from the deferential young man.

"Have you ever been in Stockholm?"

"No, Excellency."

"Or in any of the German ports?"

"No, Excellency."

"Do you know where we are making for now?"

"No, Excellency."

"Nor when we shall reach our destination?"

"No, Excellency."

"You have some prisoners aboard?"

"Three drunken sailors, Excellency."

"Yes, that's what the Captain said. But if it meant death for a sailor to be drunk, the commerce of the world would speedily stop."

"This is a government steamer, Excellency, and if a sailor here disobeys orders he is guilty of mutiny. On a merchant vessel they would merely put him in irons."

"I see. Now do you want to earn a few gold pieces?"

"Excellency has been very generous to me already," was the non-committal reply of the steward, whose eyes nevertheless twinkled at the mention of gold.

"Well, here's enough to make a jingle in your pocket, and here are two letters which you are to try to get delivered when you return to St. Petersburg."

"Yes, Excellency."

"You will do your best?"

"Yes, Excellency."

"Well, if you succeed, I'll make your fortune when I'm released."

"Thank you, Excellency."

That night at dinner the Captain opened a bottle of vodka, and conversed genially on many topics, without touching upon the particular subject of liberty. He partook sparingly of the stimulant, and, to Lermontoff's disappointment, it did not in the least loosen his tongue, and thus, still ignorant of his fate, the Prince turned in for the second night aboard the steamer.

When he awoke next morning he found the engines had stopped, and, as the vessel was motionless, surmised it had reached harbor. He heard the intermittent chuck-chuck of a pony engine, and the screech of an imperfectly-oiled crane, and guessed that cargo was being put ashore.

"Now," he said to himself, "if my former sentinel is at the door they are going to take me to prison. If he is absent, I am to be set free."

He jumped up, threw back the bolt, opened the door. There was no one there. In a very few minutes he was on deck, and found that the steamer was lying in the lee of a huge rock, which reminded him of Mont St. Michel in Normandy, except that it was about half again as high, and three times as long, and that there were no buildings of any kind upon it, nor, indeed, the least sign of human habitation.

The morning was fine; in the east the sun had just risen, and was flooding the grim rock with a rosy light. Except this rock, no trace of land was visible as far as the eye could see. Alongside the steamer was moored a sailing-boat with two masts, but provided also with thole-pins, and sweeps for rowing. The sails were furled, and she had evidently been brought to the steamer's side by means of the oars. Into this craft the crane was lowering boxes, bags, and what-not, which three or four men were stowing away. The mate was superintending this transshipment, and the Captain, standing with his back against the deck-house, was handing one by one certain papers, which Lermontoff took to be bills of lading, to a young man who signed in a book for each he received. When this transaction was completed, the young man saluted the Captain, and descended over the ship's side to the sail-boat.

"Good morning, Captain. At anchor, I see," said Lermontoff.

"No, not at anchor. Merely lying here. The sea is too deep, and affords no anchorage at this point."

"Where are all these goods going?"

The Captain nodded his head at the rock, and Lermontoff gazed at it again, running his eyes from top to bottom without seeing any vestige of civilization.

"Then you lie to the lee of this rock, and the small boat takes the supplies ashore?"

"Exactly," said the Captain.

"The settlement, I take it, is on the other side. What is it—a lighthouse?"

"There's no lighthouse," said the Captain.

"Sort of coastguard, then?"

"Yes, in a way. They keep a lookout. And now, Highness, I see your overcoat is on your back. Have you left anything in your room?"

The Prince laughed.

"No, Captain, I forgot to bring a portmanteau with me."

"Then I must say farewell to you here."

"What, you are not going to maroon me on this pebble in the ocean?"

"You will be well taken care of, Highness."

"What place is this?"

"It is called the Trogzmondoff, Highness, and the water surrounding you is the Baltic."

"Is it Russian territory?"

"Very, very Russian," returned the Captain drawing a deep breath. "This way, if your Highness pleases. There is a rope ladder, which is sometimes a little unsteady for a landsman, so be careful."

"Oh, I'm accustomed to rope ladders. Hyvasti, Captain."

"Hyvasti, your Highness."

And with this mutual good-by in Finnish, the Prince went down the swaying ladder.

# CHAPTER XV — "A HOME ON THE ROLLING DEEP"

FOR once the humorous expression had vanished from Captain Kempt's face, and that good-natured man sat in the dainty drawing-room of the flat a picture of perplexity. Dorothy had told him the story of the Nihilist, saying she intended to purchase the yacht, and outlining what she proposed to do with it when it was her own. Now she sat silent opposite the genial Captain, while Katherine stood by the window, and talked enough for two, sometimes waxing indignant, and occasionally giving, in terse language, an opinion of her father, as is the blessed privilege of every girl born in the land of the free, while the father took the censure with the unprotesting mildness of his nature.

"My dear girls, you really must listen to reason. What you propose to do is so absurd that it doesn't even admit of argument. Why, it's a filibustering expedition, that's what it is. You girls are as crazy as Walker of Nicaragua. Do you imagine that a retired Captain of the United States Navy is going to take command of a pirate craft of far less legal standing than the 'Alabama,' for then we were at war, but now we are at peace. Do you actually propose to attack the domain of a friendly country! Oh!" cried the Captain, with a mighty explosion of breath, for at this point his supply of language entirely gave out.

"No one would know anything about it," persisted Katherine.

"Not know about it? With a crew of men picked up here in New York, and coming back to New York? Not know about it? Bless my soul, the papers would be full of it before your men were an hour on shore. In the first place, you'd never find the rock."

"Then what's the harm of going in search of it?" demanded his daughter. "Besides that, Johnson knows exactly where it is."

"Johnson, Johnson! You're surely not silly enough to believe Johnson's cock-and-bull story?"

"I believe every syllable he uttered. The man's face showed that he was speaking the truth."

"But, my dear Kate, you didn't see him at all, as I understand the yarn. He was here alone with you, was he not, Dorothy?"

Dorothy smiled sadly.

"I told Kate all about it, and gave my own impression of the man's appearance."

"You are too sensible a girl to place any credit in what he said, surely?"

"I did believe him, nevertheless," replied Dorothy.

"Why, look you here. False in one thing, false in all. I'll just take a single point. He speaks of a spring sending water through the cells up there in the rock. Now, that is an impossibility. Wherever a spring exists, it comes from a source higher than itself."

"There are lots of springs up in the mountains," interrupted Katherine. "I know one on Mount Washington that is ten times as high as the rock in the Baltic."

"Quite so, Katherine, quite so, but nevertheless there is a lake, subterraneous or above ground, which feeds your White Mountain spring, and such a lake must be situated higher than the spring is. Why, girl, you ought to study hydrometeorology as well as chemistry. Here is a rock jutting up in midocean—"

"It's in the Baltic, near the Russian coast," snapped Kate, "and I've no doubt there are mountains in Finland that contain the lake which feeds the spring."

"How far is that rock from the Finnish coast, then?"

"Two miles and a half," said Kate, quick as an arrow speeding from a bow.

"Captain, we don't know how far it is from the coast," amended Dorothy.

"I'll never believe the thing exists at all."

"Why, yes it does, father. How can you speak like that? Don't you know Lieutenant Drummond fired at it?"

"How do you know it was the same rock?"

"Because the rock fired back at him. There can't be two like that in the Baltic."

"No, nor one either," said the Captain, nearing the end of his patience.

"Captain Kempt," said Dorothy very soothingly, as if she desired to quell the rising storm, "you take the allegation about the spring of water to prove that Johnson was telling untruths. I expect him here within an hour, and I will arrange that you have an opportunity, privately, of cross-examining him. I think when you see the man, and listen to him, you will believe. What makes me so sure that he is telling the truth is the fact that he mentioned the foreign vessel firing at this rock, which I knew to be true, and which he could not possibly have learned anything about."

"He might very well have learned all particulars from the papers, Dorothy. They were full enough of the subject at the time, and, remembering this, he thought to strengthen his story by—"

Katherine interrupted with great scorn.

"By adding verisimilitude to an otherwise bald and unconvincing narrative."

"Quite so, Kate; exactly what I was going to say myself. But to come back to the project itself. Granting the existence of the rock, granting the truth of Johnson's story, granting everything, granting even that the young men are imprisoned there, of which we have not the slightest proof, we could no more succeed in capturing that place from a frail pleasure yacht—"

"It's built like a cruiser," said Katherine.

"Even if it were built like a battleship we would have no chance whatever. Why, that rock might defy a regular fleet. Our venture would simply be a marine Jameson Raid which would set the whole world laughing when people came to hear of it."

"Johnson said he could take it with half a dozen men."

"No, Kate," corrected Dorothy, "he said the very reverse; that two or three determined men on the rock with repeating rifles could defeat a host. It was I who suggested that we should throw a shell, and then rush the entrance in the confusion."

Captain Kempt threw up his hands in a gesture of despair.

"Great heavens, Dorothy Amhurst, whom I have always regarded as the mildest, sweetest and most charming of girls; to hear you calmly propose to throw a shell among a lot of innocent men defending their own territory against a perfectly unauthorized invasion! Throw a shell, say you, as if you were talking of tossing a copper to a beggar! Oh, Lord, I'm growing old. What will become of this younger generation? Well, I give it up. Dorothy, my dear, whatever will happen to those unfortunate Russians, I shall never recover from the shock of your shell. The thing is absolutely impossible. Can't you see that the moment you get down to details? How are you going to procure your shells, or your shell-firing gun? They are not to be bought at the first hardware store you come to on Sixth Avenue."

"Johnson says he can get them," proclaimed Kate with finality.

"Oh, damn Johnson! Dorothy, I beg your pardon, but really, this daughter of mine, combined with that Johnson of yours, is just a little more than I can bear."

"Then what are we to do?" demanded his daughter. "Sit here with folded hands?"

"That would be a great deal better than what you propose. You should do something sane. You mustn't involve a pair of friendly countries in war. Of course the United States would utterly disclaim your act, and discredit me if I were lunatic enough to undertake such a wild goose chase, which I'm not; but, on the other hand, if two of our girls undertook such an expedition, no man can predict the public clamor that might arise. Why, when the newspapers get hold of a question, you never know where they will end it. Undoubtedly you two girls should be sent to prison, and, with equal undoubtedness, the American people wouldn't permit it."

"You bet they wouldn't," said Katherine, dropping into slang.

"Well, then, if they wouldn't, there's war."

"One moment, Captain Kempt," said Dorothy, again in her mildest tones, for voices had again begun to run high, "you spoke of doing something sane. You understand the situation. What should you counsel us to do?"

The Captain drew a long breath, and leaned back in his chair.

"There, Dad, it's up to you," said Katherine. "Let us hear your proposal, and then you'll learn how easy it is to criticise."

"Well," said the Captain hesitatingly, "there's our diplomatic service—"

"Utterly useless: one man is a Russian, and the other an Englishman. Diplomacy not only can do nothing, but won't even try," cried Kate triumphantly.

"Yet," said the Captain, with little confidence, "although the two men are foreigners, the two girls are Americans."

"We don't count: we've no votes," said Kate. "Besides, Dorothy tried the diplomatic service, and could not even get accurate information from it. Now, father, third time and out."

"Four balls are out, Kate, and I've only fanned the air twice. Now, girls, I'll tell you what I'd do. You two come with me to Washington. We will seek a private interview with the President. He will get into communication with the Czar, also privately, and outside of all regular channels. The Czar will put machinery in motion that is sure to produce those two young men much more effectually and speedily than any cutthroat expedition on a yacht."

"I think," said Dorothy, "that is an excellent plan."

"Of course it is," cried the Captain enthusiastically. "Don't you see the pull the President will have? Why, they've put an Englishman into 'the jug,' and when the President communicates this fact to the Czar he will be afraid to refuse, knowing that the next appeal may be from America to England, and when you add a couple of American girls to that political mix-up, why, what chance has the Czar?"

"The point you raise, Captain," said Dorothy, "is one I wish to say a few words about. The President cannot get Mr. Drummond released, because the Czar and all his government will be compelled to deny that they know anything of him. Even the President couldn't guarantee that the Englishman would keep silence if he were set at liberty. The Czar would know that, but your plan would undoubtedly produce Prince Ivan Lermontoff. All the president has to do is to tell the Czar that the Prince is engaged to an American girl, and Lermontoff will be allowed to go."

"But," objected the Captain, "as the Prince knows the Englishman is in prison, how could they be sure of John keeping quiet when Drummond is his best friend?"

"He cannot know that, because the Prince was arrested several days before Drummond was.

"They have probably chucked them both into the same cell," said the Captain, but Dorothy shook her head.

"If they had intended to do that, they would doubtless have arrested them together. I am sure that one does not know the fate of the other, therefore the Czar can quite readily let Lermontoff go, and he is certain to do that at a word from the President. Besides this, I am as confident that Jack is not in the Trogzmondoff, as I am sure that Drummond is. Johnson said it was a prison for foreigners."

"Oh, Dorothy," cried the Captain, with a deep sigh, "if we've got back again to Johnson—" He waved his hand and shook his head.

The maid opened the door and said, looking at Dorothy:

"Mr. Paterson and Mr. Johnson."

"Just show them into the morning room," said Dorothy, rising. "Captain

144

Kempt, it is awfully good of you to have listened so patiently to a scheme of which you couldn't possibly approve."

"Patiently!" sniffed the daughter.

"Now I want you to do me another kindness."

She went to the desk and picked up a piece of paper.

"Here is a check I have signed—a blank check. I wish you to buy the yacht 'Walrus' just as she stands, and make the best bargain you can for me. A man is so much better at this kind of negotiation than a woman."

"But surely, my dear Dorothy, you won't persist in buying this yacht?"

"It's her own money, father," put in Katherine.

"Keep quiet," said the Captain, rising, for the first time speaking with real severity, whereupon Katherine, in spite of the fact that she was older than twenty-one, was wise enough to obey.

"Yes, I am quite determined, Captain," said Dorothy sweetly.

"But, my dear woman, don't you see how you've been hoodwinked by this man Johnson? He is shy of a job. He has already swindled you out of twenty thousand dollars."

"No, he asked for ten only, Captain Kempt, and I voluntarily doubled the amount."

"Nevertheless, he has worked you up to believe that these young men are in that rock. He has done this for a very crafty purpose, and his purpose seems likely to succeed. He knows he will be well paid, and you have promised him a bonus besides. If he, with his Captain Kidd crew, gets you on that yacht, you will only step ashore by giving him every penny you possess. That's his object. He knows you are starting out to commit a crime—that's the word, Dorothy, there's no use in our mincing matters—you will be perfectly helpless in his hands. Of course, I could not allow my daughter Kate to go on such an expedition."

"I am over twenty-one years old," cried Kate, the light of rebellion in her eyes.

"I do not intend that either of you shall go, Katherine."

"Dorothy, I'll not submit to that," cried Katherine, with a rising tremor of anger in her voice, "I shall not be set aside like a child. Who has more at stake than I? And as for capturing the rock, I'll dynamite it myself, and bring home as large a specimen of it as the yacht will carry, and set it up on Bedloe's Island beside the Goddess and say, 'There's your statue of Liberty, and there's your statue of Tyranny!'"

"Katherine," chided her father, "I never before believed that a child of mine could talk such driveling nonsense."

"Paternal heredity, father," retorted Kate.

"Your Presidential plan, Captain Kempt," interposed Dorothy, "is excellent so far as Prince Lermontoff is concerned, but it cannot rescue Lieutenant Drummond. Now, there are two things you can do for me that will make me always your debtor, as, indeed, I am already, and the first is to purchase for me the yacht. The second is to form your own judgment of the man Johnson, and if you distrust him, then engage for me one-half the crew, and see that they are picked Americans."

"First sane idea I have heard since I came into this flat," growled the Captain.

"The Americans won't let the Finlander hold me for ransom, you may depend upon that."

It was a woe-begone look the gallant Captain cast on the demure and determined maiden, then, feeling his daughter's eye upon him, he turned toward her.

"I'm going, father," she said, with a firmness quite equal to his own, and he on his part recognized when his daughter had toed the danger line. He indulged in a laugh that had little of mirth in it.

"All I can say is that I am thankful you haven't made up your minds to kidnap the Czar. Of course you are going, Kate, So am I."

146

# CHAPTER XVI —CELL NUMBER NINE

AS the sailing-boat cast off, and was shoved away from the side of the steamer, there were eight men aboard. Six grasped the oars, and the young clerk who had signed for the documents given to him by the Captain took the rudder, motioning Lermontoff to a seat beside him. All the forward part of the boat, and, indeed, the space well back toward the stern, was piled with boxes and bags.

"What is this place called?" asked the Prince, but the young steersman did not reply.

Tying the boat to iron rings at the small landing where the steps began, three of the men shipped their oars. Each threw a bag over his shoulder, walked up half a dozen steps and waited. The clerk motioned Lermontoff to follow, so he stepped on the shelf of rock and looked upward at the rugged stairway cut between the main island and an outstanding perpendicular ledge of rock. The steps were so narrow that the procession had to move up in Indian file; three men with bags, then the Prince and the clerk, followed by three more men with boxes. Lermontoff counted two hundred and thirty-seven steps, which brought him to an elevated platform, projecting from a doorway cut in the living rock, but shielded from all sight of the sea. The eastern sun shone through this doorway, but did not illumine sufficiently the large room whose walls, ceiling and floor were of solid stone. At the farther end a man in uniform sat behind a long table on which burned an oil lamp with a green shade. At his right hand stood a broad, round brazier containing glowing coals, after the Oriental fashion, and the officer was holding his two hands over it, and rubbing them together. The room, nevertheless, struck chill as a cellar, and Lermontoff heard a constant smothered roar of water.

The clerk, stepping forward and saluting, presented to the Governor seated there the papers and envelopes given him by the Captain. The officer selected a blue sheet of paper, and scrutinized it for a moment under the lamp.

"Where are the others?"

"We have landed first the supplies, Governor; then the boat will return for the others."

The Governor nodded, and struck a bell with his open palm. There entered a big man with a bunch of keys at his belt, followed by another who carried a lighted lantern.

"Number Nine," said the Governor to the gaolers.

"I beg your pardon, sir, am I a prisoner?" asked Lermontoff.

The Governor gave utterance to a sound that was more like the grunt of a pig than the ejaculation of a man. He did not answer, but looked up at the questioner, and the latter saw that his face, gaunt almost as that of a living skeleton, was pallid as putty.

"Number Nine," he repeated, whereupon the gaoler and the man with the lantern put a hand each on Lermontoff's shoulders, and marched him away. They walked together down a long passage, the swaying lantern casting its yellow rays on the iron bolts of door after door, until at last the gaoler stopped, threw back six bolts, inserted a key, unlocked the door, and pushed it ponderously open. The lantern showed it to be built like the door of a safe, but unlike that of a safe it opened inwards. As soon as the door came ajar Lermontoff heard the sound of flowing water, and when the three entered, he noticed a rapid little stream sparkling in the rays of the lantern at the further end of the cell. He saw a shelf of rock and a stone bench before it. The gaoler placed his hands on a black loaf, while the other held up the lantern.

"That will last you four days," said the gaoler.

"Well, my son, judging from the unappetizing look of it, I think it will last me much longer."

The gaoler made no reply, but he and the man with the lantern retired, drawing the door heavily after them. Lermontoff heard the bolts thrust into place, and the turn of the key; then silence fell, all but the babbling of the water. He stood still in the center of the cell, his hands thrust deep in the pockets of his overcoat, and, in spite of this heavy garment, he shivered a little.

"Jack, my boy," he muttered, "this is a new deal, as they say in the West. I can imagine a man going crazy here, if it wasn't for that stream. I never knew what darkness meant before. Well, let's find out the size of our kingdom."

He groped for the wall, and stumbling against the stone bench, whose existence he had forgotten, pitched head forward to the table, and sent the four-day loaf rolling on the floor. He made an ineffectual grasp after the loaf, fearing it might fall into the stream and be lost to him, but he could not find it, and now his designs for measuring the cell gave place to the desire of finding that loaf. He got down on his hands and knees, and felt the stone floor inch by inch for half an hour, as he estimated the time, but never once did he touch the bread.

"How helpless a man is in the dark, after all," he muttered to himself. "I must do this systematically, beginning at the edge of the stream."

On all fours he reached the margin of the rivulet, and felt his way along the brink till his head struck the opposite wall. He turned round, took up a position that he guessed was three feet nearer the door, and again traversed the room, becoming so eager in the search that he forgot for the moment the horror of his situation, just as, when engaged in a chemical experiment, everything else vanished from his mind, and thus after several journeys back and forth he was again reminded of the existence of the stone bench by butting against it when he knew he was still several feet from the wall. Rubbing his head, he muttered some unfavorable phrases regarding the immovable bench, then crawled round it twice, and resumed his transverse excursions. At last he reached the wall that held the door, and now with breathless eagerness rubbed his shoulder against it till he came to the opposite corner. He knew he had touched with knees and hands practically every square inch of space in the floor, and yet no bread.

"Now, that's a disaster," cried he, getting up on his feet, and stretching himself. "Still, a man doesn't starve in four days. I've cast my bread on the waters. It has evidently gone down the stream. Now, what's to hinder a man escaping by means of that watercourse? Still, if he did, what would be the use? He'd float out into the Baltic Sea, and if able to swim round the rock, would merely be compelled to knock at the front door and beg admission again. No, by Jove, there's the boat, but they probably guard it night and day, and a man in the water would have no chance against one in the boat. Perhaps there's gratings between the cells. Of course, there's bound to be. No one would leave the bed of a stream clear for any one to navigate. Prisoners would visit each other in their cells, and that's not allowed in any respectable prison. I wonder if there's any one next door on either side of me. An iron grid won't keep out the sound. I'll try," and going again to the margin of the watercourse, he shouted several times as loudly as he could, but only a sepulchral echo, as if from a vault, replied to him.

"I imagine the adjoining cells are empty. No enjoyable companionship to be expected here. I wonder if they've got the other poor devils up from the steamer yet. I'll sit down on the bench and listen."

He could have found the bench and shelf almost immediately by groping round the wall, but he determined to exercise his sense of direction, to pit himself against the darkness.

"I need not hurry," he said, "I may be a long time here."

In his mind he had a picture of the cell, but now that he listened to the water it seemed to have changed its direction, and he found he had to rearrange this mental picture, and make a different set of calculations to fit the new position. Then he shuffled slowly forward with hands outstretched, but he came to the wall, and not to the bench. Again he mapped out his route, again endeavored, and again failed.

"This is bewildering," he muttered. "How the darkness baffles a man. For the first time in my life I appreciate to the full the benediction of God's command, 'Let there be light.'"

He stood perplexed for a few moments, and, deeply thinking, his hands automatically performed an operation as the servants of habit. They took from his pocket his cigarette case, selected a tube of tobacco, placed it between his lips, searched another pocket, brought out a match-box, and struck a light. The striking of the match startled Lermontoff as if it had been an explosion; then he laughed, holding the match above his head, and there at his feet saw the loaf of black bread. It seemed as if somebody had twisted the room end for end. The door was where he thought the stream was, and thus he learned that sound gives no indication of direction to a man blindfolded. The match began to wane, and feverishly he lit his cigarette.

"Why didn't I think of the matches, and oh! what a pity I failed to fill my pockets with them that night of the Professor's dinner party! To think that matches are selling at this moment in Sweden two hundred and fifty for a halfpenny!"

Guided by the spark at the end of his cigarette, he sought the bench and sat down upon it. He was surprised to find himself so little depressed as was actually the case. He did not feel in the least disheartened. Something was going to happen on his behalf; of that he was quite certain. It was perfectly ridiculous that even in Russia a loyal subject, who had never done any illegal act in his life, a nobleman of the empire, and a friend of the Czar, should be incarcerated for long without trial, and even without accusation. He had no enemies that he knew of, and many friends, and yet he experienced a vague uneasiness when he remembered that his own course of life had been such that he would not be missed by his friends. For more than a year he had been in England, at sea, and in America, so much absorbed in his researches that he had written no private letters worth speaking of, and if any friend were asked his whereabouts, he was likely to reply:

"Oh, Lermontoff is in some German university town, or in England, or traveling elsewhere. I haven't seen him or heard of him for months. Lost in a wilderness or in an experiment, perhaps."

These unhappy meditations were interrupted by the clang of bolts. He thought at first it was his own door that was being opened, but a moment later knew it was the door of the next cell up-stream. The sound, of course, could not penetrate the extremely thick wall, but came through the aperture whose roof arched the watercourse. From the voices he estimated that several

151

prisoners were being put into one cell, and he wondered whether or not he cared for a companion. It would all depend. If fellow-prisoners hated each other, their enforced proximity might prove unpleasant.

"We are hungry," he heard one say. "Bring us food."

The gaoler laughed.

"I will give you something to drink first."

"That's right," three voices shouted. "Vodka, vodka!"

Then the door clanged shut again, and he heard the murmur of voices in Russian, but could not make out what was said. One of the new prisoners, groping round, appeared to have struck the stone bench, as he himself had done. The man in the next cell swore coarsely, and Lermontoff, judging from such snatches of their conversation as he could hear that they were persons of a low order, felt no desire to make their more intimate acquaintance, and so did not shout to them, as he had intended to do. And now he missed something that had become familiar; thought it was a cigarette he desired, for the one he had lit had been smoked to his very lips, then he recognized it was the murmur of the stream that had ceased.

"Ah, they can shut it off," he said. "That's interesting. I must investigate, and learn whether or no there is communication between the cells. Not very likely, though."

He crawled on hands and knees until he came to the bed of the stream, which was now damp, but empty. Kneeling down in its course, he worked his way toward the lower cell, and, as he expected, came to stout iron bars. Crouching thus he sacrificed a second match, and estimated that the distance between the two cells was as much as ten feet of solid rock, and saw also that behind the perpendicular iron bars were another horizontal set, then another perpendicular, then a fourth horizontal.

While in this position he was startled by a piercing scream to the rear. He backed out from the tunnel and stood upright once more. He heard the sound of people splashing round in water. The screamer began to jabber

152

like a maniac, punctuating his ravings with shrieks. Another was cursing vehemently, and a third appealing to the saints. Lermontoff quickly knelt down in the watercourse, this time facing the upper cell, and struck his third match. He saw that a steel shield, reminding him of the thin shutter between the lenses of a camera, had been shot across the tunnel behind the second group of cross bars, and as an engineer he could not but admire the skill of the practical expert who had constructed this diabolical device, for in spite of the pressure on the other side, hardly a drop of water oozed through. He tried to reach this shield, but could not. It was just beyond the touch of his fingers, with his arm thrust through the two sets of bars, but if he could have stretched that far, with the first bar retarding his shoulder, he knew his hand would be helpless even if he had some weapon to puncture the steel shield. The men would be drowned before he could accomplish anything unless he was at the lever in the passage outside.

Crawling into his cell again he heard no more of the chatter and cries of the maniac, and he surmised that the other two were fighting for places on bench or shelf, which was amply large enough to have supported both, had they not been too demented with fear to recognize that fact. The cursing man was victorious, and now he stood alone on the shelf, roaring maledictions. Then there was the sound of a plunge, and Lermontoff, standing there, helpless and shivering, heard the prisoner swim round and round his cell like a furious animal, muttering and swearing.

"Don't exhaust yourself like that," shouted Lermontoff. "If you want to live, cling to the hole at either of the two upper corners. The water can't rise above you then, and you can breathe till it subsides."

The other either did not hear, or did not heed, but tore round and round in his confined tank, thrashing the water like a dying whale.

"Poor devil," moaned Jack. "What's the use of telling him what to do. He is doomed in any case. The other two are now better off."

A moment later the water began to dribble through the upper aperture into Jack's cell, increasing and increasing until there was the roar of a waterfall, and he felt the cold splashing drops spurt against him. Beyond this there was silence. It was perhaps ten minutes after that the lever was pulled, and the water belched forth from the lower tunnel like a mill race broken loose, temporarily flooding the floor so that Jack was compelled to stand on the bench.

He sunk down shivering on the stone shelf, laid his arms on the stone pillow, and buried his face in them.

"My God, my God!" he groaned.

# CHAPTER XVII — A FELLOW SCIENTIST

IN this position Jack slept off and on, or rather, dozed into a kind of semi-stupor, from which he awoke with a start now and then, as he thought he heard again the mingled cries of devotion and malediction. At last he slept soundly, and awoke refreshed, but hungry. The loaf lay beside him, and with his knife he cut a slice from it, munching the coarse bread with more of relish than he had thought possible when he first saw it. Then he took out another cigarette, struck a match, looked at his watch, and lit the cigarette. It was ten minutes past two. He wondered if a night had intervened, but thought it unlikely. He had landed very early in the morning, and now it was afternoon. He was fearfully thirsty, but could not bring himself to drink from that stream of death. Once more he heard the bolts shot back.

"They are going to throw the poor wretches into the sea," he muttered, but the yellow gleam of a lantern showed him it was his own door that had been unlocked.

"You are to see the Governor," said the gaoler gruffly. "Come with me."

Jack sprang to the floor of his cell, repressing a cry of delight. Nothing the grim Governor could do to him would make his situation any worse, and perhaps his persuasive powers upon that official might result in some amelioration of his position. In any case there was the brief respite of the interview, and he would gladly have chummed with the devil himself to be free a few moments from this black pit.

Although the outside door of the Governor's room stood open, the room was not as well illumined as it had been before, for the sun had now gone round to the other side of the island, but to the prisoner's aching eyes it seemed a chamber of refulgence. The same lamp was burning on the table, giving forth an odor of bad oil, but in addition to this, two candles were lighted, which supplemented in some slight measure the efforts of the lamp. At the end of the table lay a number of documents under a paper-weight, arranged with the neat precision of a methodical man. The Governor had been warming his hands over the brazier, but ceased when Lermontoff was brought up standing before him. He lifted the paper-weight, took from under it the two letters which Lermontoff had given to the steward on the steamer, and handed them to the prisoner, who thus received them back for the second time.

"I wish to say," remarked the Governor, with an air of bored indifference which was evidently quite genuine, "that if you make any further attempt to communicate with the authorities, or with friends, you will bring on yourself punishment which will be unpleasant."

"As a subject of the Czar, I have the right to appeal to him," said the Prince.

"The appeal you have written here," replied the Governor, "would have proved useless, even if it had been delivered. The Czar knows nothing of the Trogzmondoff, which is a stronghold entirely under the control of the Grand Dukes and of the Navy. The Trogzmondoff never gives up a prisoner."

"Then I am here for a lifetime?"

"Yes," rejoined the Governor, with frigid calmness, "and if you give me no trouble you will save yourself some inconvenience."

"Do you speak French?" asked the Prince.

"Net."

"English?"

"Net."

"Italian?"

"Net."

"German?"

"Da."

"Then," continued Lermontoff in German, "I desire to say a few words to you which I don't wish this gaoler to understand. I am Prince Ivan Lermontoff, a personal friend of the Czar's, who, after all, is master of the Grand Dukes and the Navy also. If you will help to put me into communication with him, I will guarantee that no harm comes to you, and furthermore will make you a rich man."

The Governor slowly shook his head.

"What you ask is impossible. Riches are nothing to me. Bribery may do much in other parts of the Empire, but it is powerless in the Trogzmondoff. I shall die in the room adjoining this, as my predecessor died. I am quite as much a prisoner in the Trogzmondoff as is your Highness. No man who has once set foot in this room, either as Governor, employee, or prisoner, is allowed to see the mainland again, and thus the secret has been well kept. We have had many prisoners of equal rank with your Highness, friends of the Czar too, I dare say, but they all died on the Rock, and were buried in the Baltic."

"May I not be permitted to receive certain supplies if I pay for them? That is allowed in other prisons."

The Governor shook his head.

"I can let you have a blanket," he said, "and a pillow, or a sheepskin if you find it cold at first, but my power here is very limited, and, as I tell you, the officers have little more comfort than the prisoners."

"Oh, I don't care anything about comfort," protested Lermontoff. "What I want is some scientific apparatus. I am a student of science. I have nothing to do with politics, and have never been implicated in any plot. Someone in authority has made a stupid mistake, and so I am here. This mistake I am quite certain will be discovered and remedied. I hold no malice, and will say nothing of the place, once I am free. It is no business of mine. But I do not wish to have the intervening time wasted. I should like to buy some electrical machinery, and materials, for which I am willing to pay any price that is asked."

"Do you understand electricity?" questioned the Governor, and for the first time his impassive face showed a glimmer of interest.

"Do I understand electricity? Why, for over a year I have been chief electrician on a war-ship."

"Perhaps then," said the Governor, relapsing into Russian again, "you can tell me what is wrong with our dynamo here in the Rock. After repeated requisition they sent machinery for lighting our offices and passages with electricity. They apparently did not care to send an electrician to the Trogzmondoff, but forwarded instead some books of instruction. I have been working at it for two years and a half, but I am still using oil lamps and candles. We wired the place without difficulty." He held up the candle, and showed, depending from the ceiling, a chandelier of electric lamps which Lermontoff had not hitherto noticed, various brackets, and one or two stand lamps in a corner, with green silk-covered wire attached.

"May I see your dynamo?" asked Lermontoff.

The Governor, with one final warming of his hands, took up a candle, told the gaoler to remove the shade from the lamp and bring it, led the way along a passage, and then into a room where the prisoner, on first entering, had heard the roar of water.

"What's this you have. A turbine? Does it give you any power?"

"Oh, it gives power enough," said the Governor.

"Let's see how you turn on the stream."

The Governor set the turbine at work, and the dynamo began to hum, a sound which, to the educated ear of Lermontoff, told him several things.

"That's all right, Governor, turn it off. This is a somewhat old-fashioned dynamo, but it ought to give you all the light you can use. You must be a natural born electrician, or you never could have got this machinery working as well as it does."

The dull eyes of the Governor glowed for one brief moment, then resumed their customary expression of saddened tiredness.

"Now," said Jack, throwing off his coat, "I want a wrench, screwdriver, hammer and a pair of pincers if you've got them."

"Here is the tool chest," said the Governor, and Jack found all he needed. Bidding the Governor hold the candle here, there and elsewhere, and ordering the gaoler about as if he were an apprentice, Jack set energetically to work, and for half an hour no one spoke.

"Turn on that water again," he commanded.

The Governor did so, and the machine whirred with quite a different note. Half a dozen electric lamps in the room flooded the place with a dazzling white glow.

"There you are," cried Jack, rubbing the oil off his hands on a piece of coarse sacking. "Now, Tommy, put these things back in the tool chest," he said to the gaoler. Then to the Governor:

"Let's see how things look in the big room."

The passage was lit, and the Governor's room showed every mark on wall, ceiling and floor.

"I told you, Governor," said Jack with a laugh, "that I didn't know why I was sent here, but now I understand. Providence took pity on you, and ordered me to strike a light."

At that moment the gaoler entered with his jingling keys, and the enthusiastic expression faded from the Governor's face, leaving it once more coldly impassive, but he spoke in German instead of Russian.

"I am very much indebted to your Highness, and it grieves me that our relationship remains unchanged."

"Oh, that's all right," cried Lermontoff breezily, "If it is within your power to allow me to come and give you some lessons in electricity and the care of dynamos, I shall be very glad to do so."

To this offer the Governor made no reply, but he went on still in German.

"I shall transfer you to cell Number One, which is not only more comfortable, but the water there is pure. Did you say you spoke English?"

"Yes, quite as well as I do Russian."

The Governor continued, with nevertheless a little hesitation: "On the return of the steamer there will be an English prisoner. I will give him cell Number Two, and if you don't talk so loud that the gaoler hears you, it may perhaps make the day less wearisome."

"You are very kind," said Jack, rigidly suppressing any trace of either emotion or interest as he heard the intelligence; leaping at once to certain conclusions, nevertheless. "I shan't ask for anything more, much as I should like to mention candles, matches, and tobacco."

"It is possible you may find all three in Number One before this time to-morrow;" then in Russian the Governor said to the goaler:

"See if Number One is ready."

The gaoler departed, and the Governor, throwing open a drawer in his table, took out two candles, a box of matches, and a packet of cigarettes.

"Put these in your pocket," he said. "The cell door opens very slowly, so you will always know when the gaoler is coming. In that case blow out your light and conceal your candle. It will last the longer."

The gaoler returned.

"The cell is ready, Excellency," he said.

"Take away the prisoner," commanded the Governor, gruffly.

# CHAPTER XVIII — CELL NUMBER ONE

CELL Number One was a great improvement on Number Nine. There was no shelf of rock, or stone bench, but a cot bed in the corner, a table, and a wooden chair. The living spring issued from the living rock in a corner of the room. When the gaoler and his assistant had retired and shoved in the outside bolts, Jack lit his candle and a cigarette, feeling almost happy. He surveyed the premises now with more care. The bed was of iron and fastened to the floor. On the top of it was a mattress, a pillow, and a pair of blankets. At its head a little triangular shelf of rock had been left in the corner, and on this reposed a basin of tin, while a coarse piece of sacking took the place of a towel. Jack threw off his overcoat and flung it on the bed, intent on a satisfactory wash. He heard something jingle in the pockets, and forgetting for the moment what it could possibly be, thrust his hand in, and pulled out a glass-stoppered bottle of ozak. He held it out at arm's length, and stared at it for some moments like a man hypnotized.

"Holy Saint Peter!" he cried, "to think that I should have forgotten this!"

He filled the tin basin with water, and placed it on the table. Again he dissolved a minute portion of the chemical, and again filled the syringe.

"I must leave no marks on the wall that may arouse attention," he said, and taking the full syringe to the arch over the torrent, and placing the candle on the floor beside him, he gently pushed in the piston. The spray struck the rock, and the rock dissolved slightly but perceptibly. Coming back to the table he stood for a few minutes in deep thought. Although the cot bed was fixed to the floor, and although it was possible that the shelf in the next cell coincided with its position, the risk of discovery was too great to cut a passage between the two cells there. The obvious spot to attack was the interior of the tunnel through which the streamlet ran, but Jack, testing the temperature of the water with his hand, doubted his physical ability to remain in that ice-cold current more than a few minutes at a time, and if he worked in the tunnel he would be all but submerged. He feared he would perish with cold and cramp before he had made any impression on the rock.

To the edge of the stream he drew the table, and, mounting it, examined the upper orifice through which the water escaped when the cell was full. He found he could stand on the table and work in comfort until he had excavated sufficient rock to allow him to clamber into the upper tunnel and so continue his operations. The water he used would flow through the tunnel, and down to the main stream in the next cell. All he had to do was to dissolve a semi-circular hole in the rock that would bend round the end of those steel bars, and enter the tunnel again on the other side. Eager to be at work, he took the full basin, shoved it far along the tunnel until it was stopped by the bars, then, placing his candle beside it, and standing on the table, he began operations.

The limestone, under the influence of the spray, dissolved very slowly, and by the time the basin of water was exhausted, all the effect visible under the light of the candle was an exceedingly slight circular impression which was barely visible to the naked eye.

"I must make the solution stronger, I think," he said, grievously disappointed at the outcome of his labors, and as he looked at it he heard the clank of the withdrawing bolts. Blowing out the candle he sprang to the floor of the cell, picked up the table, set it down in the center of the room, groped for the chair, and sat down, his heart palpitating wildly at the fear of discovery.

Followed as usual by the man with the lantern, the gaoler came in, carrying a bowl of hot steaming soup, which he placed on the table, then he took from his pocket a spoon, a small hunk of black bread, and a piece of cheese. In the light of the lantern Lermontoff consulted his watch, and found it was six o'clock. The gaoler took the lantern from his assistant, held it high, and looked round the room, while Lermontoff gazed at him in anxiety, wondering whether that brutal looking official suspected anything. Apparently he did not, but merely wished to satisfy himself that everything was in order, for he said more mildly than he had hitherto spoken:

"It is a long time since any one occupied this cell."

Then his eye rested on the vacant corner shelf.

"Ah, Excellency," he continued, "pardon me, I have forgotten. I must bring you a basin."

"I'd rather you brought me a candle," said Lermontoff nonchalantly, although his lips were dry, and he moistened them as he spoke; then, to learn whether money was valueless on the rock, as the Governor had intimated, he drew from his pocket one of the remaining gold pieces, glad that he happened to have so many, and slipped it into the palm of the gaoler's hand, whose fingers clutched it as eagerly as if he were in St. Petersburg.

"I think a candle can be managed, Excellency. Shall I bring a cup?"

"I wish you would."

The door was again locked and bolted, but before Lermontoff had finished his soup, and bread and cheese, it was opened again. The gaoler placed a tin basin, similar to the former one, on the ledge, put a candle and a candle-stick on the table, and a tin cup beside them.

"I thought there was no part of Russia where bribery was extinct," said the Prince to himself, as the door closed again for the night.

After supper Lermontoff again shined his table, stood upon it, lit his candle, and resumed his tunnelling, working hard until after midnight. His progress was deplorably slow, and the spraying of the rock proved about as tiring a task as ever he had undertaken. His second basin-full of solution was made a little stronger, but without perceptible improvement, in its effect. On ceasing operations for the night he found himself in a situation common to few prisoners, that of being embarrassed with riches. He possessed two basins, and one of them must be concealed. Of course he might leave his working basin in the upper tunnel where it had rested when the gaoler had brought in his supper, but he realized that at any moment the lantern's rays might strike its shining surface, and so bring on an investigation of the upper tunnel, certain to prove the destruction of his whole scheme. A few minutes thought, however, solved the problem admirably: he placed the basin face downwards in the rapid stream which swept it to the iron bars between the two cells, and there it lay quite concealed with the swift water rippling over it. This done, he flung off his clothes, and got into bed, not awakening until the gaoler and his assistant brought in bread, cheese and coffee for breakfast.

The next day he began to feel the inconveniences of the Governor's friendship, and wished he were safely back to the time when one loaf lasted four days, for if such were now the case, he would be free of the constant state of tension which the ever-recurring visits of the gaoler caused. He feared that some day he might become so absorbed in his occupation that he would not hear the withdrawing of the bolt, and thus, as it were, be caught in the act.

Shortly after lunch the Governor sent for him, and asked many questions pertaining to the running of the dynamo. Lermontoff concealed his impatience, and set about his instructions with exemplary earnestness. Russian text books on electricity at hand were of the most rudimentary description, and although the Governor could speak German he could not read it, so the two volumes he possessed in that language were closed to him. Therefore John was compelled to begin at the very A B C of the science.

The Governor, however, became so deeply interested that he momentarily forgot his caution, unlocked a door, and took Lermontoff into a room which he saw was the armory and ammunition store-house of the prison. On the floor of this chamber the Governor pointed out a large battery of accumulators, and asked what they were for. Lermontoff explained the purposes of the battery, meanwhile examining it thoroughly, and finding that many of the cells had been all but ruined in transit, through the falling away of the composition in the grids. Something like half of the accumulators, however, were intact and workable; these he uncoupled and brought into the dynamo room, where he showed the Governor the process of charging. He saw in the store room a box containing incandescent lamps, coils of silk-covered wire and other material that made his eyes glisten with delight. He spoke in German.

"If you will give me a coil of this wire, one or two of the lamps, and an accumulator, or indeed half a dozen of them, I will trouble you no more for candles."

The Governor did not reply at the moment, but a short time after asked

Lermontoff in Russian how long it would be before the accumulators were charged. Lermontoff stated the time, and the Governor told the gaoler to bring the prisoner from the cell at that hour, and so dismissed his instructor.

One feature of this interview which pleased Lermontoff was that however much the Governor became absorbed in these lessons, he never allowed himself to remain alone with his prisoner. It was evident that in his cooler moments the Governor had instructed the gaoler and his assistant to keep ever at the heels of the Prince and always on the alert. Two huge revolvers were thrust underneath the belt of the gaoler, and the lantern-holder, was similarly armed. Lermontoff was pleased with this, for if the Governor had trusted him entirely, even though he demanded no verbal parole, it would have gone against his grain to strike down the chief as he ruthlessly intended to do when the time was ripe for it, and in any case, he told himself, no matter how friendly the Governor might be, he had the misfortune to stand between his prisoner and liberty.

Lermontoff was again taken from his cell about half an hour before the time he had named for the completion of the charging, and although the Governor said nothing of his intention, the gaoler and his man brought to the cell six charged batteries, a coil of wire, and a dozen lamps. Lermontoff now changed his working methods. He began each night as soon as he had finished dinner, and worked till nearly morning, sleeping all day except when interrupted by the gaoler. Jack, following the example of Robinson Crusoe, attempted to tie knots on the tail of time by cutting notches with his knife on the leg of the table, but most days he forgot to perform this operation, and so his wooden almanac fell hopelessly out of gear. He estimated that he had been a little more than a week in prison when he heard by the clang of the bolts that the next cell was to have an occupant.

"I must prepare a welcome for him," he said, and so turned out the electric light at the end of the long flexible wire. He had arranged a neat little switch of the accumulator, and so snapped the light on and off at his pleasure, without the trouble of unscrewing the nuts which held in place one of the copper ends of the wire. Going to the edge of the stream and lighting his candle, he placed the glass bulb in the current, paid out the flexible line attached to it, and allowed the bulb to run the risk of being smashed against the iron bars of the passage, but the little globe negotiated the rapids without even a perceptible clink, and came to rest in the bed of the torrent somewhere about the center of the next cell, tugging like a fish on a hook. Then Jack mounted the table, leaned into the upper tunnel, and listened.

"I protest," Drummond cried, speaking loudly, as if the volume of sound would convey meaning to alien ears, "I protest against this as an outrage, and demand my right of communication with the British Ambassador."

Jack heard the gaoler growl: "This loaf of bread will last you for four days," but as this statement was made in Russian, it conveyed no more meaning to the Englishman than had his own protest of a moment before brought intelligence to the gaoler. The door clanged shut, and there followed a dead silence.

"Now we ought to hear some good old British oaths," said Jack to himself, but the silence continued.

"Hullo, Alan," cried Jack through the bars, "I said you would be nabbed if you didn't leave St. Petersburg. You'll pay attention to me next time I warn you."

There was no reply, and Jack became alarmed at the continued stillness, then he heard his friend mutter:

"I'll be seeing visions by and by. I thought my brain was stronger than it is—could have sworn that was Jack's voice."

Jack got speedily and quietly down, turned on the switch, and hopped up on the table again, peering through. He knew that the stream had now become a river of fire, and that it was sending to the ceiling an unholy, unearthly glow.

"Oh, damn it all!" groaned Drummond, at which Jack roared with laughter.

"Alan," he shouted, "fish out that electric bulb from the creek and hold it aloft; then you'll see where you are. I'm in the next cell; Jack Lamont,

166

Electrician and Coppersmith: all orders promptly attended to: best of references, and prices satisfactory."

"Jack, is that really you, or have I gone demented?"

"Oh, you always were demented, Alan, but it is I, right enough. Pick up the light and tell me what kind of a cell you've got."

"Horrible!" cried Drummond, surveying his situation. "Walls apparently of solid rock, and this uncanny stream running across the floor."

"How are you furnished? Shelf of rock, stone bench?"

"No, there's a table, cot bed, and a wooden chair."

"Why, my dear man, what are you growling about? They have given you one of the best rooms in the hotel. You're in the Star Chamber."

"Where in the name of heaven are we?"

"Didn't you recognize the rock from the deck of a steamer?"

"I never saw the deck of a steamer."

"Then how did you come here?"

"I was writing a letter in my room when someone threw a sack over my head, and tied me up in a bundle, so that it was a close shave I wasn't smothered. I was taken in what I suppose was a cab and flung into what I afterwards learned was the hold of a steamer. When the ship stopped, I was carried like a sack of meal on someone's shoulder, and unhampered before a gaunt specter in uniform, in a room so dazzling with electric light that I could hardly see. That was a few minutes ago, Now I am here, and starving. Where is this prison?"

"Like the Mikado, as Kate would say, the authorities are bent on making the punishment fit the crime. You are in the rock of the Baltic, which you fired at with that gun of yours. I told you those suave officials at St. Petersburg were playing with you."

"But why have they put you here, Jack?"

167

"Oh, I was like the good dog Tray, who associated with questionable company, I suppose, and thus got into trouble."

"I'm sorry."

"You ought to be glad. I'm going to get out of this place, and I don't believe you could break gaol, unassisted, in twenty years. Here is where science confronts brutality. I say, Drummond, bring your table over to the corner, and mount it, then we can talk without shouting. Not much chance of any one outside hearing us, even if we do clamor, but this is a damp situation, and loud talk is bad for the throat. Cut a slice of that brown bread and lunch with me. You'll find it not half bad, as you say in England, especially when you are hungry. Now," continued Jack, as his friend stood opposite him, and they found by experiment that their combined reach was not long enough to enable them to shake hands through the bars, "now, while you are luxuriating in the menu of the Trogzmondoff, I'll give you a sketch of my plan for escape."

"Do," said Drummond.

"I happen to have with me a pair of bottles containing a substance which, if dissolved in water, and sprinkled on this rock, will disintegrate it. It proves rather slow work, I must admit, but I intend to float in to you one of the bottles, and the apparatus, so that you may help me on your side, which plan has the advantage of giving you useful occupation, and allowing us to complete our task in half the time, like the engineers on each side of the Simplon Tunnel."

"If there are bars in the lower watercourse," objected Drummond, "won't you run a risk of breaking your bottle against them?"

"Not the slightest. I have just sent that much thinner electric lamp through, but in this case I'll just tie up the bottle and squirt gun in my stocking, attach that to the wire, and the current will do the rest. You can unload, and I'll pull my stocking back again. If I dared wrench off a table leg, I could perhaps shove bottle and syringe through to you from here, but the material would come to a dead center in the middle of this tunnel, unless I had a stick to push it within your reach.

"Very well; we'll work away until our excavation connects, and we have made it of sufficient diameter for you to squeeze through. You are then in my cell. We put out our lights, and you conceal yourself behind the door. Gaoler and man with the lantern come in. You must be very careful not to close the door, because if you once shove it shut we can't open it from this side, even though it is unlocked and the bolts drawn. It fits like wax, and almost hermetically seals the room. You spring forward, and deal the gaoler with your fist one of your justly celebrated English knock-down blows, immediately after felling the man with the lantern. Knowing something of the weight of your blow, I take it that neither of the two men will recover consciousness until we have taken off their outer garments, secured revolvers and keys. Then we lock them in, you and I on the outside."

"My dear Jack, we don't need any tunnel to accomplish that. The first time these two men come into my room, I can knock them down as easily here as there."

"I thought of that, and perhaps you could, but you must remember we have only one shot. If you made a mistake; if the lantern man bolted and fired his pistol, and once closed the door—he would not need to pause to lock it—why, we are done for. I should be perfectly helpless in the next room, and after the attempt they'd either drown us, or put us into worse cells as far apart as possible."

"I don't think I should miss fire," said Drummond, confidently, "still, I see the point, and will obey orders."

"My official position on the rock, ever since I arrived, has been that of electrical tutor-in-chief to the Governor. I have started his dynamo working, and have wired such portions of the place as were not already wired before. During these lessons I have kept my eyes open. So far as the prison is concerned, there is the Governor, a sort of head clerk, the gaoler and his assistant; four men, and that is all. The gaoler's assistant appears to be the cook of the place, although the cooking done is of the most limited description. The black bread is brought from St. Petersburg, I think, as also tinned meat and soup; so the cuisine is on a somewhat limited scale."

169

"Do you mean to say that only these four men are in charge of the prison?"

"Practically so, but there is the garrison as well. The soldiers live in a suite of rooms directly above us, and as near as I can form an opinion, there are fourteen men and two officers. When a steamer arrives they draft as many soldiers as are necessary, unload the boat; then the Tommies go upstairs again. The military section apparently holds little intercourse with the officials, whom they look upon as gaolers. I should judge that the military officer is chief of the rock, because when he found the Governor's room lit by electricity, he demanded the same for his quarters. That's how I came to get upstairs. Now, these stairs are hewn in the rock, are circular, guarded by heavy oaken doors top and bottom, and these doors possess steel bolts on both sides of them. It is thus possible for either the military authorities upstairs, or the civil authorities, to isolate themselves from the others. In case of a revolt among the soldiers, the Governor could bolt them into their attic, and they would find great difficulty in getting out. Now, my plan of procedure is this. We will disarm gaoler and assistant, take their keys, outside garments and caps. The gaoler's toggery will fit you, and the other fellow's may do for me. Then we will lock them in here, and if we meet clerk or Governor in the passages we will have time to overcome either or both before they are aware of the change. I'll go up the circular stair, bolt from the inside the upper door, and afterwards bolt the lower door. Then we open all the cells, and release the other prisoners, descend from the rock, get into the Finnish fishing boat, keep clear of the two cannon that are up above us, and sail for the Swedish coast. We can't miss it; we have only to travel west, and ultimately we are safe. There is only one danger, which is that we may make our attempt when the steamer is here, but we must chance that."

"Isn't there any way of finding out? Couldn't you pump the Governor?"

"He is always very much on his guard, and is a taciturn man. The moment the tunnel is finished I shall question him about some further electrical material, and then perhaps I may get a hint about the steamer. I imagine she comes irregularly, so the only safe plan would be for us to make our attempt just after she had departed."

"Would there be any chance of our finding a number of the military downstairs?"

"I don't think so. Now that they have their electric light they spend their time playing cards and drinking vodka."

"Very well, Jack, that scheme seems reasonably feasible. Now, get through your material to me, and issue your instructions."

## CHAPTER XIX —"STONE WALLS DO NOT A PRISON MAKE"

IN a very short time Drummond became as expert at the rock dissolving as was his friend. He called it piffling slow work, but was nevertheless extremely industrious at it, although days and weeks and, as they suspected, months, passed before the hands of the two friends met in the center of the rock. One lucky circumstance that favored them was the habit of the gaoler in visiting Drummond only once every four days.

The Lieutenant made his difficult passage, squeezing through the newly completed tunnel half an hour after a loaf had been set upon his table. Jack knew that the steamer had recently departed, because, two days before, the Governor had sent for him, and had exhibited a quantity of material recently landed, among other things a number of electric bells and telephones which the Governor was going to have set up between himself and the others, and also between his room and that of the clerk and gaoler. There were dry batteries, and primary batteries, and many odds and ends, which made Jack almost sorry he was leaving the place.

Heavy steps, muffled by the thickness of the door, sounded along the outer passage.

"Ready?" whispered Jack. "Here they come. Remember if you miss your first blow, we're goners, you and I."

Drummond made no reply, for the steps had come perilously near and he feared to be heard. Noiselessly he crossed the cell and took up his position against the wall, just clear of the space that would be covered by the opening of the door.

At the same moment Jack switched off the light, leaving the room black. Each of the two waiting prisoners could hear the other's short breathing through the darkness.

On came the shuffling footsteps of the gaoler and lantern-bearer. They had reached the door of Number One, had paused, had passed on and stopped in front of Number Two.

"Your cell!" whispered Jack, panic-stricken. "And they weren't due to look in on you for four days. It's all up! They'll discover the cell is empty and give the—Where are you going, man?" he broke off, as Drummond, leaving his place near the door, groped his way hurriedly along the wall.

"To squeeze my way back and make a fight for it. It's better than—"

"Wait!"

Lamont's hand was on his shoulder, and he whispered a sharp command for silence. The two attendants had halted in front of Number Two, and while the lantern-bearer fumbled with the awkward bolt, his companion was saying:

"Hold on! After all, I'll bring the other his food first, I think."

"But," remonstrated the lantern-bearer, "the Governor said we were to bring the Englishman to him at once."

"What if he did? How will he know we stole a half minute to give the Prince his dinner? If we bring the Englishman upstairs first, the Prince may have to wait an hour before we can get back with the Englishman."

"Let him wait, then."

"With his pocket full of roubles? Not I. He may decide to give no more of his gold pieces to a gaoler who lets him go hungry too long."

"I've got the door unfastened now and—"

"Then fasten it again and come back with me to Number One."

Faint as were the words, deadened by intervening walls, their purport reached Jack.

"Back to your place," he whispered, "they're coming!"

The rattle of bolts followed close on his words. The great door of Number One swung ponderously inward. The lantern-bearer, holding his light high in front of him, entered; then stepped to one side to admit the gaoler, who came close after, the tray of food in his outstretched hands.

Unluckily for the captives' plan, it was to the side of the cell opposite to that where Alan crouched that the lantern-bearer had taken his stand. There was no way of reaching him at a bound. The open door stood between. Were the gaoler to be attacked first, his fellow-attendant could readily be out of the cell and half-way up the corridor before Alan might hope to reach him.

The friends had counted on both men entering the room together and crossing as usual to the table. This change of plan disconcerted them. Already the gaoler had set down his tray and was turning toward the door. Alan, helpless, stood impotently in the shadow, biting his blond mustache with helpless rage. In another second their cherished opportunity would vanish. And, as the gaoler's next visit was to be to Number Two, discovery stared them in the eyes.

It was Jack who broke the momentary spell of apathy. He was standing at the far end of the cell, near the stream.

"Here!" he called sharply to the lantern-bearer, "bring your light. My electric apparatus is out of order, and I've mislaid my matches. I want to fix—"

The lantern-bearer, obediently, had advanced into the room. He was half-way across it while Lamont was still speaking. Then, from the corner of his eye, he spied Alan crouching in the angle behind the door, now fully exposed to the rays of the lantern.

The man whirled about in alarm just as Alan sprang. In consequence the Englishman's mighty fist whizzed past his head, missing it by a full inch.

The gaoler, recovering from his amaze, whipped out one of the revolvers he wore in his belt. But Jack, leaping forward, knocked it from his hand before he could fire; and, with one hand clapped across the fellow's bearded lips, wound his other arm about the stalwart body so as to prevent for the instant the drawing of the second pistol.

Alan's first blow had missed clean; but his second did not. Following up his right-hand blow with all a trained boxer's swift dexterity, he sent a straight left hander flush on the angle of the light-bearer's jaw. The man dropped his lantern and collapsed into a senseless heap on the floor, while Alan, with no further delay, rushed toward the gaoler.

The fall of the lantern extinguished the light. The cell was again plunged in dense blackness, through which could be heard the panting and scuffing of the Prince and the gaoler.

Barely a second of time had elapsed since first Jack had seized the man, but that second had sufficed for the latter to summon his great brute strength and shake off his less gigantic opponent and to draw his pistol.

"Quick, Alan!" gasped Jack. "He's got away from me. He'll—"

Drummond, guided by his friend's voice, darted forward through the darkness, caught his foot against the sprawling body of the lantern-bearer and fell heavily, his arms thrown out in an instinctive gesture of self-preservation. Even as he lost his balance he heard a sharp click, directly in front of him. The gaoler had pulled the trigger, and his pistol—contract-made and out of order, like many of the weapons of common soldiers in Russia's frontier posts—had missed fire.

To that luckiest of mishaps, the failure of a defective cartridge to explode, the friends owed their momentary safety.

As Alan pitched forward, one of his outing arms struck against an obstacle. It was a human figure, and from the feel of the leather straps, which his fingers touched in the impact, he knew it was the gaoler and not Lamont.

Old football tactics coming to memory, Alan clung to the man his arm had chanced upon, and bore him along to the ground; Jack, who had pressed forward in the darkness, being carried down as well by the other's fall.

Gaoler, Prince and Englishman thus struggled on the stone floor in one indistinguishable heap. It was no ordinary combat of two to one, for neither of the prisoners could say which was the gaoler and which his friend. The gaoler, troubled by no such doubts, laid about him lustily, and was only prevented from crying out by the fact that his heavy fur cap had, in the fall, become jammed down over his face as far as the chin and could not for the moment be dislodged.

He reached for and drew the sword-bayonet that hung at his side (for his second pistol had become lost in the scrimmage), and thrust blindly about him. Once, twice his blade met resistance and struck into flesh.

"Jack," panted Alan, "the beast's stabbing. Get yourself loose and find the electric light."

As he spoke, Alan's hand found the gaoler's throat. He knew it was not Alan's from the rough beard that covered it. The gaoler, maddened by the pressure, stabbed with fresh fury; most of his blows, fortunately, going wild in the darkness.

Alan's free hand reached for and located the arm that was wielding the bayonet, and for a moment the two wrestled desperately for its possession.

Then a key clicked, and the room was flooded with incandescent light, just as Alan, releasing his grip on the Russian's throat, dealt him a short-arm blow on the chin with all the power of his practiced muscles. The gaoler relaxed his tense limbs and lay still, while Alan, bleeding and exhausted, struggled to his feet.

"Hot work, eh?" he panted. "Hard position to land a knockout from. But I caught him just right. He'll trouble us no more for a few minutes, I fancy. You're bleeding! Did he wound you?"

"Only a scratch along my check. And you?"

"A cut on the wrist and another on the shoulder, I think. Neither of them bad, thanks to the lack of aim in the dark. Close call, that! Now to tie them up. Not a movement from either yet."

"You must have come close to killing them with those sledge-hammer blows of yours!"

"It doesn't much matter," said the imperturbable pugilist, "they'll be all right in half an hour. It's knowing where to hit. If there are only four men downstairs, we don't need to wear the clothes of these beasts. Let us take only the bunch of keys and the revolvers."

Securing these the two stepped out into the passage, locked and bolted the door; then Jack, who knew his way, proceeded along the passage to the stairway, leaped nimbly up the steps, bolted the door leading to the military quarters, then descended and bolted the bottom door.

"Now for the clerk, and then for the Governor."

The clerk's room connected with the armory, which was reached by passing through the apartment that held turbine and dynamo, which they found purring away merrily.

Covering the frightened clerk with four revolvers, Jack told him in Russian that if he made a sound it would be his last. They took him, opened cell Number Three, which was empty, and thrust him in.

Jangling the keys, the two entered the Governor's room. The ancient man looked up, but not a muscle of his face changed; even his fishy eyes showed no signs of emotion or surprise.

"Governor," said Jack with deference, "although you are under the muzzles of a quartet of revolvers, no harm is intended you. However, you must not leave your place until you accompany us down to the boat, when I shall hand the keys over to you, and in cell Number One you will find gaoler and lantern man a little worse for wear, perhaps, but still in the ring, I hope. In Number Three your clerk is awaiting you. I go now to release your prisoners. All communication between yourself and the military is barred. I leave my friend on guard until I return from the cells. You must not attempt to summon assistance, or cry out, or move from your chair. My friend does not understand either Russian or German, so there is no use in making any appeal to him, and much as I like you personally, and admire your assiduity in science, our case is so desperate that if you make any motion whatever, he will be compelled to shoot you dead."

The Governor bowed.

"May I continue my writing?" he asked.

Jack laughed heartily.

"Certainly," and with that he departed to the cells, which he unlocked one by one, only to find them all empty.

Returning, he said to the Governor:

"Why did you not tell me that we were your only prisoners?"

"I feared," replied the Governor mildly, "that you might not believe me."

"After all, I don't know that I should,", said Jack, holding out his hand, which the other shook rather unresponsively.

"I want to thank you," the Governor said slowly, "for all you have told me about electricity. That knowledge I expect to put to many useful purposes in the future, and the exercise of it will also make the hours drag less slowly than they did before you came."

"Oh, that's all right," cried Jack with enthusiasm. "I am sure you are very welcome to what teaching I have been able to give you, and no teacher could have wished a more apt pupil."

"It pleases me to hear you say that, Highness, although I fear I have been lax in my duties, and perhaps the knowledge of this place which you have got through my negligence, has assisted you in making an escape which I had not thought possible."

Jack laughed good-naturedly.

"All's fair in love and war," he said. "Imprisonment is a section of war. I must admit that electricity has been a powerful aid to us. But you cannot blame yourself, Governor, for you always took every precaution, and the gaoler was eternally at my heels. You can never pretend that you trusted me, you know."

"I tried to do my duty," said the old man mournfully, "and if electricity has been your helper, it has not been with my sanction. However, there is one point about electricity which you impressed upon me, which is that although it goes quickly, there is always a return current."

"What do you mean by that, Governor?"

"Is it not so? It goes by a wire, and returns through the earth. I thought you told me that."

"Yes, but I don't quite see why you mention that feature of the case at this particular moment."

"I wanted to be sure what I have stated is true. You see, when you are gone there will be nobody I can ask."

All this time the aged Governor was holding Jack's hand rather limply. Drummond showed signs of impatience.

"Jack," he cried at last, "that conversation may be very interesting, but it's like smoking on a powder mine. One never knows what may happen. I shan't feel safe until we're well out at sea, and not even then. Get through with your farewells as soon as possible, and let us be off."

"Right you are, Alan, my boy. Well, Governor, I'm reluctantly compelled to bid you a final good-by, but here's wishing you all sorts of luck."

The old man seemed reluctant to part with him, and still clung to his hand.

"I wanted to tell you," he said, "of another incident, almost as startling as your coming into this room a while since, that happened six or eight months ago. As perhaps you know, we keep a Finland fishing-boat down in the cove below."

"Yes, yes," said Jack impatiently, drawing away his hand.

"Well, six or eight months ago that boat disappeared, and has never been heard of since. None of our prisoners was missing; none of the garrison was missing; my three assistants were still here, yet in the night the boat was taken away."

"Really. How interesting! Never learned the secret, did you?"

179

"Never, but I took precautions, when we got the next boat, that it should be better guarded, so I have had two men remain upon it night and day."

"Are your two men armed, Governor?"

"Yes, they are."

"Then they must surrender, or we will be compelled to shoot them. Come down with us, and advise them to surrender quietly, otherwise, from safe cover on the stairway, we can pot them in an open boat."

"I will go down with you," said the Governor, "and do what I can."

"Of course they will obey you."

"Yes, they will obey me—if they hear me. I was going to add that only yesterday did I arrange the electric bell down at the landing, with instructions to those men to take a telegram which I had written in case of emergencies, to the mainland, at any moment, night or day, when that bell rang. Your Highness, the bell rang more than half an hour ago. I have not been allowed out to see the result."

The placid old man put his hand on the Prince's shoulder, as if bestowing a benediction upon him. Drummond, who did not understand the lingo, was amazed to see Jack fling off the Governor's grasp, and with what he took to be a crushing oath in Russian, spring to the door, which he threw open. He mounted the stone bench which gave him a view of the sea. A boat, with two sails spread, speeding to the southwest, across the strong westerly wind, was two miles or more away.

"Marooned, by God!" cried the Prince, swinging round and presenting his pistol at the head of the Governor, who stood there like a statue of dejection, and made no sign.

# CHAPTER XX —ARRIVAL OF THE TURBINE YACHT

BEFORE Jack could fire, as perhaps he had intended to do, Drummond struck down his arm.

"None of that, Jack," he said. "The Russian in you has evidently been scratched, and the Tartar has come uppermost. The Governor gave a signal, I suppose?"

"Yes, he did, and those two have got away while I stood babbling here, feeling a sympathy for the old villain. That's his return current, eh?"

"He's not to blame," said Drummond. "It's our own fault entirely. The first thing to have done was to secure that boat."

"And everything worked so beautifully," moaned Jack, "up to this point, and one mistake ruins it. We are doomed, Alan."

"It isn't so bad as that, Jack," said the Englishman calmly. "Should those men reach the coast safely, as no doubt they will, it may cost Russia a bit of trouble to dislodge us."

"Why, hang it all," cried Jack, "they don't need to dislodge us. All they've got to do is to stand off and starve us out. They are not compelled to fire a gun or land a man."

"They'll have to starve their own men first. It's not likely we're going to go hungry and feed our prisoners."

"Oh, we don't mind a little thing like that, we Russians. They may send help, or they may not. Probably a cruiser will come within hailing distance and try to find out what the trouble is. Then it will lie off and wait till everybody's dead, and after that put in a new Governor and another garrison."

"You take too pessimistic a view, Jack. This isn't the season of the year for a cruiser to lie off in the Baltic. Winter is coming on. Most of the harbors in Finland will be ice-closed in a month, and there's no shelter hereabouts in a storm. They'll attack; probably open shell fire on us for a while, then attempt to land a storming party. That will be fun for us if you've got good rifles and plenty of ammunition."

Jack raised his head.

"Oh, we're well-equipped," he said, "if we only have enough to eat."

Springing to his feet, all dejection gone, he said to the Governor:

"Now, my friend, we're compelled to put you into a cell. I'm sorry to do this, but there is no other course open. Where is your larder, and what quantity of provisions have you in stock?"

A gloomy smile added to the dejection of the old man's countenance.

"You must find that out for yourself," he said.

"Are the soldiers upstairs well supplied with food?"

"I will not answer any of your questions."

"Oh, very well. I see you are determined to go hungry yourself. Until I am satisfied that there is more than sufficient for my friend and me, no prisoner in my charge gets anything to eat. That's the sort of gaoler I am. The stubborn old beast!" he cried in English, turning to Drummond, "won't answer my questions."

"What were you asking him?"

"I want to know about the stock of provisions."

"It's quite unnecessary to ask about the grub: there's sure to be ample."

"Why?"

"Why? Because we have reached the beginning of winter, as I said before. There must be months when no boat can land at this rock. It's bound to be provisioned for several months ahead at the very lowest calculation. Now, the first thing to do is to put this ancient Johnny in his little cell, then I'll tell you where our chief danger lies."

182

The Governor made neither protest nor complaint, but walked into Number Nine, and was locked up.

"Now, Johnny, my boy," said Drummond, "our anxiety is the soldiers. The moment they find they are locked in they will blow those two doors open in just about half a jiffy. We can, of course, by sitting in front of the lower door night and day, pick off the first four or five who come down, but if the rest make a rush we are bound to be overpowered. They have, presumably, plenty of powder, probably some live shells, petards, and what-not, that will make short work even of those oaken doors. What do you propose to do?"

"I propose," said Jack, "to fill their crooked stairway with cement. There are bags and bags of it in the armory."

The necessity for this was prevented by an odd circumstance. The two young men were seated in the Governor's room, when at his table a telephone bell rang. Jack had not noticed this instrument, and now took up the receiver.

"Hello, Governor," said a voice, "your fool of a gaoler has bolted the stairway door, and we can't open it."

"Oh, I beg pardon," replied Jack, in whatever imitation of the Governor's voice he could assume. "I'll see to it at once myself."

He hung up the receiver and told his comrade what had happened.

"One or both of these officers are coming down. If we get the officers safely into a cell, there will be nobody to command the men, and it is more than likely that the officers carry the keys of the powder room. I'll turn out the electric lamps in the hall, and light the lantern. You be ready at the foot of the stairway to fire if they make the slightest resistance."

The two officers came down the circular stairway, grumbling at the delay to which they had been put. Lermontoff took advantage of the clamping of their heavy boots in the echoing stairway to shove in the bolts once more, and then followed them, himself followed by Drummond, into the Governor's room. Switching on the electric light, he said:

"Gentlemen, I am Prince Lermontoff, in temporary charge of this prison. The Governor is under arrest, and I regret that I must demand your swords, although I have every reason to believe that they will be handed back to you within a very few days after I have completed my investigations."

The officers were too much accustomed to sudden changes in command to see anything odd in this turn of affairs. Lermontoff spoke with a quiet dignity that was very convincing, and the language he used was that of the nobility. The two officers handed him their swords without a word of protest.

"I must ask you whether you have yet received your winter supply of food."

"Oh, yes," said the senior officer, "we had that nearly a month ago."

"Is it stored in the military portion of the rock, or below here?"

"Our rations are packed away in a room upstairs."

"I am sorry, gentlemen, that I must put you into cells until my mission is accomplished. If you will write a requisition for such rations as you are accustomed to receive, I shall see that you are supplied. Meanwhile, write also an order to whomsoever you entrust in command of the men during your absence, to grant no one leave to come downstairs, and ask him to take care that each soldier is rigidly restricted to the minimum quantity of vodka."

The senior officer sat down at the table, and wrote the two orders. The men were then placed in adjoining cells, without the thought of resistance even occurring to them. They supposed there had been some changes at headquarters, and were rather relieved to have the assurance of the Prince that their arrest would prove temporary. Further investigation showed that there would be no danger of starvation for six months at least.

Next day Jack, at great risk of his neck, scaled to the apex of the island, as he had thought of flying, if possible, a signal of distress that might attract some passing vessel. But even though he reached the sharp ridge, he saw at once that no pole could be erected there, not even if he possessed one. The wind aloft was terrific, and he gazed around him at an empty sea.

When four days had passed they began to look for the Russian relief boat, which they knew would set out the moment the Governor's telegram reached St. Petersburg.

On the fifth day Jack shouted down to Drummond, who was standing by the door.

"The Russian is coming: heading direct for us. She's in a hurry, too, crowding on all steam, and eating up the distance like a torpedo-boat destroyer. I think it's a cruiser. It's not the old tub I came on, anyway."

"Come down, then," answered Alan, "and we—"

A cry from above interrupted him. Jack, having at first glance spied the vessel whose description he had shouted to Drummond, had now turned his eyes eastward and stood staring aghast toward the sunrise.

"What's the matter?" asked Alan.

"Matter?" echoed Jack. "They must be sending the whole Russian Navy here in detachments to capture our unworthy selves. There's a second boat coming from the east—nearer by two miles than the yacht. If I hadn't been all taken up with the other from the moment I climbed here I'd have seen her before."

"Is she a yacht, too?"

"No. Looks like a passenger tramp. Dirty and—"

"Merchantman, maybe."

"No. She's got guns on her—"

"Merchantman fitted out for privateersman, probably. That's the sort of craft Russia would be likeliest to send to a secret prison like this. What flag does—"

"No flag at all. Neither of them. They're both making for the rock, full steam, and from opposite sides. Neither can see the other, I suppose. I—"

"From opposite sides? That doesn't look like a joint expedition. One of those ships isn't Russian. But which?"

Jack had clambered down and stood by Alan's side.

"We must make ready for defense in either case," he said. "In a few minutes we'll be able to see them both from the platform below."

"One of those boats means to blow us out of existence if it can," mused Jack. "The other cannot know of our existence. And yet, if she doesn't, what is she doing here, headed for the rock?"

With that Jack scrambled, slid and jumped down. Drummond was very quiet and serious. Repeating rifles stood in a row on the opposite wall, easy to get at, but as far off as might be from the effects of a possible shell. The two young men now mounted the stone bench by the door, which allowed them to look over the ledge at the eastern sea. Presently the craft appeared round the end of the island, pure white, floating like a swan on the water, and making great headway.

"By Jove!" said Jack, "she's a fine one. Looks like the Czar's yacht, but no Russian vessel I know of can make that speed."

"She's got the ear-marks of Thornycroft build about her," commented Drummond. "By Jove, Jack, what luck if she should prove to be English. No flag flying, though."

"She's heading for us," said Jack, "and apparently she knows which side the cannon is on. If she's Russian, they've taken it for granted we've captured the whole place, and are in command of the guns. There, she's turning."

The steamer was abreast of the rock, and perhaps three miles distant. Now she swept a long, graceful curve westward and drew up about half a mile east of the rock.

"Jove, I wish I'd a pair of good glasses," said Drummond. "They're lowering a boat."

Jack showed more Highland excitement than Russian stolidity, as he watched the oncoming of a small boat, beautifully riding the waves, and masterfully rowed by sailors who understood the art. Drummond stood imperturbable as a statue.

"The sweep of those oars is English, Jack, my boy."

As the boat came nearer and nearer Jack became more and more agitated.

"I say, Alan, focus your eyes on that man at the rudder. I think my sight's failing me. Look closely. Did you ever see him before?"

"I think I have, but am not quite sure."

"Why, he looks to me like my jovial and venerable father-in-law, Captain Kempt, of Bar Harbor. Perfectly absurd, of course: it can't be."

"He does resemble the Captain, but I only saw him once or twice."

"Hooray, Captain Kempt, how are you?" shouted Jack across the waters.

The Captain raised his right hand and waved it, but made no attempt to cover the distance with his voice. Jack ran pell-mell down the steps, and Drummond followed in more leisurely fashion. The boat swung round to the landing, and Captain Kempt cried cordially:

"Hello, Prince, how are you? And that's Lieutenant Drummond, isn't it? Last time I had the pleasure of seeing you, Drummond, was that night of the ball."

"Yes," said Drummond. "I was very glad to see you then, but a hundred times happier to see you to-day."

"I was just cruising round these waters in my yacht, and I thought I'd take a look at this rock you tried to obliterate. I don't see any perceptible damage done, but what can you expect from British marksmanship?"

"I struck the rock on the other side, Captain. I think your remark is unkind, especially as I've just been praising the watermanship of your men."

"Now, are you boys tired of this summer resort?" asked Captain Kempt. "Is your baggage checked, and are you ready to go? Most seaside places are deserted this time of year."

"We'll be ready in a moment, captain," cried his future son-in-law. "I must run up and get the Governor. We've put a number of men in prison here, and they'll starve if not released. The Governor's a good old chap, though he played it low down on me a few days ago," and with that Jack disappeared up the stairway once more.

"Had a gaol-delivery here?" asked the Captain.

"Well, something by way of that. The Prince drilled a hole in the rock, and we got out. We've put the garrison in pawn, so to speak, but I've been mighty anxious these last few days because the sail-boat they had here, and two of the garrison, escaped to the mainland with the news. We were anxiously watching your yacht, fearing it was Russian. Jack thought it was the Czar's yacht. How came you by such a craft, Captain? Splendid-looking boat that."

"Oh, yes, I bought her a few days before I left New York. One likes to travel comfortably, you know. Very well fitted up she is."

Jack shouted from the doorway:

"Drummond, come up here and fling overboard these loaded rifles. We can't take any more chances. I'm going to lock up the ammunition room and take the key with me as a souvenir."

"Excuse me, Captain," said Drummond, who followed his friend, and presently bundles of rifles came clattering down the side of the precipice, plunging into the sea. The two then descended the steps, Jack in front, Drummond following with the Governor between them.

"Now, Governor," said Jack, "for the second time I am to bid you farewell. Here are the keys. If you accept them you must give me your word of honor that the boat will not be fired upon. If you do not promise that, I'll drop the bunch into the sea, and on your gray head be the consequences."

"I give you my word of honor that you shall not be fired upon."

"Very well, Governor. Here are the keys, and good-by."

In the flurry of excitement over the yacht's appearance, both Jack and Drummond had temporarily forgotten the existence of the tramp steamer the former had seen beating toward the rock.

Now Lamont suddenly recalled it.

"By the way, Governor," he said, "the relief boat you so thoughtfully sent for is on her way here. She should reach the rock at almost any minute now. In fact, I fancy we've little time to waste if we want to avoid a brush. It would be a pity to be nabbed now at the eleventh hour. Good-by, once more."

But the Governor had stepped between him and the boat.

"I—I am an old man," he said, speaking with manifest embarrassment. "I was sent to take charge of this prison as punishment for refusing to join a Jew massacre plot. Governorship here means no more nor less than a life imprisonment. My wife and children are on a little estate of mine in Sweden. It is twelve years since I have seen them. I—"

"If this story is a ruse to detain us—"

"No! No!" protested the Governor, and there was no mistaking his pathetic, eager sincerity. "But—but I shall be shot—or locked in one of the cells and the water turned on—for letting you escape. Won't you take me with you? I will work my passage. Take me as far as Stockholm. I shall be free there—free to join my wife and to live forever out of reach of the Grand Dukes. Take me—"

"Jump in!" ordered Jack, coming to a sudden resolution. "Heaven knows I would not condemn my worst enemy to a perpetual life on this rock. And you've been pretty decent to us, according to your lights. Jump aboard, we've no time to waste."

Nor did the Governor waste time in obeying. The others followed, and the boat shoved off. But scarcely had the oars caught the water when around the promontory came a large man-o'-war's launch, a rapid-fire gun mounted on her bows. She was manned by about twenty men in Russian police uniform.

"From the 'tramp,'" commented Alan excitedly. "And her gun is trained on us."

"Get down to work!" shouted Jack to the straining oarsmen.

"No use!" groaned Kempt. "She'll cross within a hundred yards of us. There's no missing at such close range and on such a quiet sea. What a fool I was to—"

The launch was, indeed, bearing down on them despite the rowers' best efforts, and must unquestionably cut them off before they could reach the yacht.

Alan drew his revolver.

"We've no earthly show against her," he remarked quietly, "and it seems hard to 'go down in sight of port.' But let's do what we can."

"Put up that pop-gun," ordered Kempt. "She will sink us long before you're in range for revolver work. I'll run up my handkerchief for a white flag."

"To surrender?"

"What else can we do?"

"And be lugged back to the rock, all of us? Not I, for one!"

The launch was now within hailing distance, and every man aboard her was glaring at the helpless little yacht-gig.

"Wait!"

It was the Governor who spoke. Rising from his seat in the stern, he hailed the officer who was sighting the rapid-fire gun.

"Lieutenant Tschersky!" he called.

At sight of the old man's lean, uniformed figure, rising from among the rest, there was visible excitement and surprise aboard the launch. The officer saluted and ordered the engine stopped that he might hear more plainly.

"Lieutenant," repeated the Governor, "I am summoned aboard His Highness the Grand Duke Vladimir's yacht. You will proceed to the harbor and await my return to the rock. There has been a mutiny among the garrison, but I have quelled it."

The officer saluted again, gave an order, and the launch's nose pointed for the rock.

"Governor," observed Lamont, as the old man sank again into his seat, "you've earned your passage to Stockholm. You need not work for it."

# CHAPTER XXI — THE ELOPEMENT

THE girls on the yacht had no expectation that Captain Kempt would come back with the two young men. But when, through their powerful binoculars, the girls became aware that Drummond and the Prince were in the small boat, they both fled to the chief saloon, and sat there holding one another's hands. Even the exuberant Kate for once had nothing to say. She heard the voice of her father on deck, giving command to the mate.

"Make for Stockholm, Johnson. Take my men-o'-war's men—see that no one else touches the ammunition—and fling the shells overboard. Heave the gun after them, and then clear out the rifles and ammunition the same way. When we reach Stockholm to-morrow morning, there must not be a gun on board this ship, and the ridiculous rumor that got abroad among your men that we were going to attack something or other, you will see is entirely unfounded. You impress that on them, Johnson."

"Oh, Dorothy," whispered Katherine, drawing a deep breath. "If you are as frightened as I am, get behind me."

"I think I will," answered Dorothy, and each squeezed the other's hand.

"I tell you what it is, Captain," sounded the confident voice of the Prince. "This vessel is a beauty. You have done yourself fine. I had no idea you were such a sybarite. Why, I've been aboard the Czar's yacht, and I tell you it's nothing—Great heavens! Katherine!" he shouted, in a voice that made the ceiling ring.

She was now standing up and advanced toward him with both hands held out, a welcoming smile on her pretty lips, but he swooped down on her, flung his arms round her like a cabman beating warmth into his hands, kissed her on the brow, the two cheeks and the lips, swaying her back and forward as if about to fling her upstairs.

"Stop, stop," she cried. "Aren't you ashamed of yourself? Before my father, too! You great Russian bear!" and, breathless, she put her open palm against his face, and shoved his head away from her.

"Don't bother about me, Kate," said her father. "That's nothing to the way we acted when I was young. Come on, boys, to the smoking-room, and I'll mix you something good: real Kentucky, twenty-seven years in barrel, and I've got all the other materials for a Manhattan."

"Jack, I am glad to see you," panted Katherine, all in disarray, which she endeavored to set right by an agitated touch here and there. "Now, Jack, I'm going to take you to the smoking-room, but you'll have to behave yourself as you walk along the deck. I won't be made a spectacle of before the crew."

"Come along, Drummond," said the Captain, "and bring Miss Dorothy with you."

But Drummond stood in front of Dorothy Amhurst, and held out his hand.

"You haven't forgotten me, Miss Amhurst, I hope?"

"Oh, no," she replied, with a very faint smile, taking his hand.

"It seems incredible that you are here," he began. "What a lucky man I am. Captain Kempt takes his yacht to rescue his son-in-law that is to be, and incidentally rescues me as well, and then to find you here! I suppose you came because your friend Miss Kempt was aboard?"

"Yes, we are all but inseparable."

"I wrote you a letter, Miss Amhurst, the last night I was in St. Petersburg in the summer."

"Yes, I received it."

"No, not this one. It was the night I was captured, and I never got a chance to post it. It was an important letter—for me."

"I thought it important—for me," replied Dorothy, now smiling quite openly. "The Nihilists got it, searching your room after you had been arrested. It was sent on to New York, and given to me."

"Is that possible? How did they know it was for you?"

"I had been making inquiries through the Nihilists."

"I wrote you a proposal of marriage, Dorothy."

"It certainly read like it, but you see it wasn't signed, and you can't be held to it."

He reached across the table, and grasped her two hands.

"Dorothy, Dorothy," he cried, "do you mean you would have cabled 'Yes'?"

"No."

"You would not?"

"Of course not. I should have cabled 'Undecided.' One gets more for one's money in sending a long word. Then I should have written—" she paused, and he cried eagerly:

"What?"

"What do you think?" she asked.

"Well, do you know, Dorothy, I am beginning to think my incredible luck will hold, and that you'd have written 'Yes.'"

"I don't know about the luck: that would have been the answer."

He sprang up, bent over her, and she, quite unaffectedly raised her face to his.

"Oh, Dorothy," he cried.

"Oh, Alan," she replied, with quivering voice, "I never thought to see you again. You cannot imagine the long agony of this voyage, and not knowing what had happened."

"It's a blessing, Dorothy, you had learned nothing about the Trogzmondoff."

"Ah, but I did: that's what frightened me. We have a man on board who was flung for dead from that dreadful rock. The Baltic saved him; his mother, he calls it."

Drummond picked her up in his arms, and carried her to the luxurious divan which ran along the side of the large room. There they sat down together, out of sight of the stairway.

"Did you get all of my letters?"

"I think so."

"You know I am a poor man?"

"I know you said so."

"Don't you consider my position poverty? I thought every one over there had a contempt for an income that didn't run into tens of thousands."

"I told you, Alan, I had been unused to money, and so your income appears to me quite sufficient."

"Then you are not afraid to trust in my future?"

"Not the least: I believe in you."

"Oh, you dear girl. If you knew how sweet that sounds! Then I may tell you. When I was in London last I ran down to Dartmouth in Devonshire. I shall be stationed there. You see, I have finished my foreign cruising, and Dartmouth is, for a time at least, to be my home. There's a fine harbor there, green hills and a beautiful river running between them, and I found such a lovely old house; not grand at all, you know, but so cosey and comfortable, standing on the heights overlooking the harbor, in an old garden filled with roses, shrubs, and every kind of flower; vines clambering about the ancient house. Two servants would keep it going like a shot. Dorothy, what do you say?"

Dorothy laughed quietly and whole heartedly.

"It reads like a bit from an old English romance. I'd just love to see such a house."

"You don't care for this sort of thing, do you?" he asked, glancing round about him.

"What sort of thing?"

"This yacht, these silk panelling, these gorgeous pictures, the carving, the gilt, the horribly expensive carpet."

"You mean should I feel it necessary to be surrounded by such luxury? I answer most emphatically, no. I like your ivy-covered house at Dartmouth much better."

For a moment neither said anything: lips cannot speak when pressed together.

"Now, Dorothy, I want you to elope with me. We will be in Stockholm long before daylight to-morrow at the rate this boat is going. I'll get ashore as soon as practicable, and make all inquiries at the consulate about being married. I don't know what the regulations are, but if it is possible to be married quietly, say in the afternoon, will you consent to that, and then write a letter to Captain Kempt, thanking him for the trip on the yacht, and I'll write, thanking him for all he has done for me, and after that we'll make for England together. I've got a letter of credit in my pocket, which luckily the Russians did not take from me. I shall find all the money we need at Stockholm, then we'll cross the Swedish country, sail to Denmark, make our way through Germany to Paris, if you like, or to London. We shan't travel all the time, but just take nice little day trips, stopping at some quaint old town every afternoon and evening."

"You mean to let Captain Kempt, Katherine, and the Prince go to America alone?"

"Of course. Why not? They don't want us, and I'm quite sure we—well, Dorothy, we'd be delighted to have them, to be sure—but still, I've knocked a good deal about Europe, and there are some delightful old towns I'd like to show you, and I hate traveling with a party."

Dorothy laughed so heartily that her head sank on his shoulder.

"Yes, I'll do that," she said at last.

And they did.

THE END

# About Author

**Early years in Canada**

Robert Barr was born in Barony, Lanark, Scotland to Robert Barr and Jane Watson. In 1854, he emigrated with his parents to Upper Canada at the age of four years old. His family settled on a farm near the village of Muirkirk. Barr assisted his father with his job as a carpenter, and developed a sound work ethic. Robert Barr then worked as a steel smelter for a number of years before he was educated at Toronto Normal School in 1873 to train as a teacher.

After graduating Toronto Normal School, Barr became a teacher, and eventually headmaster/principal of the Central School of Windsor, Ontario in 1874. While Barr worked as head master of the Central School of Windsor, Ontario, he began to contribute short stories—often based on personal experiences, and recorded his work. On August 1876, when he was 27, Robert Barr married Ontario-born Eva Bennett, who was 21. According to the 1891 England Census, the couple appears to have had three children, Laura, William, and Andrew.

In 1876, Barr quit his teaching position to become a staff member of publication, and later on became the news editor for the Detroit Free Press. Barr wrote for this newspaper under the pseudonym, "Luke Sharp." The idea for this pseudonym was inspired during his morning commute to work when Barr saw a sign that read "Luke Sharp, Undertaker." In 1881, Barr left Canada to return to England in order to start a new weekly version of "The Detroit Free Press Magazine."

**London years**

In 1881 Barr decided to "vamoose the ranch", as he called the process of immigration in search of literary fame outside of Canada, and relocated to London to continue to write/establish the weekly English edition of the Detroit Free Press. During the 1890s, he broadened his literary works, and started writing novels from the popular crime genre. In 1892 he founded the magazine The Idler, choosing Jerome K. Jerome as his collaborator (wanting, as Jerome said, "a popular name"). He retired from its co-editorship in 1895.

In London of the 1890s Barr became a more prolific author—publishing a book a year—and was familiar with many of the best-selling authors of his day, including :Arnold Bennett, Horatio Gilbert Parker, Joseph Conrad, Bret Harte, Rudyard Kipling, H. Rider Haggard, H. G. Wells, and George Robert Gissing. Barr was well-spoken, well-cultured due to travel, and considered a "socializer."

Because most of Barr's literary output was of the crime genre, his works were highly in vogue. As Sherlock Holmes stories were becoming well-known, Barr wrote and published in the Idler the first Holmes parody, "The Adventures of "Sherlaw Kombs" (1892), a spoof that was continued a decade later in another Barr story, "The Adventure of the Second Swag" (1904). Despite those jibes at the growing Holmes phenomenon, Barr remained on very good terms with its creator Arthur Conan Doyle. In Memories and Adventures, a serial memoir published 1923–24, Doyle described him as "a volcanic Anglo—or rather Scot-American, with a violent manner, a wealth of strong adjectives, and one of the kindest natures underneath it all".

In 1904, Robert Barr completed an unfinished novel for Methuen & Co. by the recently deceased American author Stephen Crane entitled The O'Ruddy, a romance. Despite his reservations at taking on the project, Barr reluctantly finished the last eight chapters due to his longstanding friendship with Crane and his common-law wife, Cora, the war correspondent and bordello owner.

### Death

The 1911 census places Robert Barr, "a writer of fiction," at Hillhead, Woldingham, Surrey, a small village southeast of London, living with his wife, Eva, their son William, and two female servants. At this home, the author died from heart disease on 21 October 1912.

### Writing Style

Barr's volumes of short stories were often written with an ironic twist in

200

the story with a witty, appealing narrator telling the story. Barr's other works also include numerous fiction and non-fiction contributions to periodicals. A few of his mystery stories and stories of the supernatural were put in anthologies, and a few novels have been republished. His writings have also attracted scholarly attention. His narrative personae also featured moral and editorial interpolations within their tales. Barr's achievements were recognized by an honorary degree from the University of Michigan in 1900.

His protagonists were journalists, princes, detectives, deserving commercial and social climbers, financiers, the new woman of bright wit and aggressive accomplishment, and lords. Often, his characters were stereotypical and romanticized.

Barr wrote fiction in an episode-like format. He developed this style when working as an editor for the newspaper Detroit Press. Barr developed his skill with the anecdote and vignette; often only the central character serves to link the nearly self-contained chapters of the novels. (Source: Wikipedia)